Meet Me On The Pier

A Holly Blue Bay Romance, Volume 4

Cathy Blossom

Published by Cathy Blossom, 2020.

Meet Me On The Pier

A Holly Blue Bay Romance

(Book 4)

By

Cathy Blossom

MEET ME ON THE PIER

First edition. March 12, 2020.

Copyright © 2020 Cathy Blossom.

ISBN: 979-8223196204

Written by Cathy Blossom.

Chapter 1

BECKY

IT WAS A BEAUTIFUL summer's day in Holly Blue Bay. Becky Carlson strolled to the end of the pier and rested her hands on the metal railings. The sun shone down on her, and a warm breeze caressed her cheek. A blue butterfly landed on the railing next to her. It was a Holly Blue one, and the town was named after the delightful creatures.

Looking out from under her straw sun hat, Becky gazed at the calm sea. A few boats bobbed leisurely on the water in seemingly no rush to get anywhere. Seagulls cried out as they circled the pier hoping for a dropped morsel of food. She heard the happy chatter of people behind her as they explored the various amusements which the pier had to offer.

Becky smiled to herself. She loved living in this town, especially on such a delightful day as today. She'd lived here all her life and couldn't imagine living anywhere else. Her job at *The Holly Blue Bay Gazette* meant she got to talk to many residents in the town even if it was only about a cracked pavement outside their house. Or a lollipop lady retiring. Or a cat stuck up a tree, which happened a surprising amount of times. She loved everything about Holly Blue Bay, but it was this pier which always filled her heart with joy.

As well as reporting on local events, Becky occasionally covered stories from residents who'd left the town but still kept it in their hearts.

She'd set up an internet notification for mentions of the town to alert her to any newsworthy items. And a notification had come up recently which Becky was excited about.

A couple called Howard and Joan Maxwell were celebrating their fiftieth wedding anniversary soon. They were both in their seventies. Joan had grown up in Holly Blue Bay and had met Howard when he'd come to the town for some reason. Becky didn't know what that reason was yet. Howard had proposed to Joan on the very pier which Becky was standing on. It was during a dance, and the couple were planning to relive that magical time by holding a dance again on their anniversary on this pier. They were going to have their family and friends along to share the celebrations.

Becky thought it was a lovely story. She'd been in touch with the couple and asked if she could meet with them to get the full details with a view to printing it in the *Gazette*. Thankfully, they had said yes. They were due to arrive today. Becky couldn't wait to hear their full story, and how they had fallen in love.

Her happiness faded a little. Perhaps their story would help heal her jaded heart. She hadn't been lucky in love and always seemed to pick the wrong man. Maybe talking to a couple who'd been married for so long would restore her faith in love.

Maybe.

Becky's thoughts turned to her love life, and all the times she'd been let down, She frowned as she recalled the lies she'd been told. Why couldn't people just be honest?

She pushed those thoughts out of her mind. They weren't welcome, and not on such a lovely day. She was looking forward to meeting the happy couple, and already had a list of questions for them.

A sudden gust took ahold of her hat and stole it from her head. Becky cried out in dismay as her sun hat danced on the wind and headed towards the water.

"Come back!" she yelled uselessly. She'd only bought that hat two days ago. It had cost more than she'd usually pay for a hat, but she hadn't been able to resist it.

And now look at it. Just flying through the air as free as a bird. She sighed as she resigned herself to never seeing her lovely hat again.

But she was wrong about that.

Chapter 2

ROBIN

FROM INSIDE HIS MOTORBOAT, Robin Hartman looked towards the shore of Holly Blue Bay. It was a pleasant town, and very picturesque. It had everything a seaside town should have. A fish and chip shop. A café. Many gift shops. Restaurants. An ice cream parlour. And the beautiful Holly Blue Hotel situated at the top of the hill. It had a magnificent view of the bay and the sea beyond. Robin was staying at the hotel whilst he was undertaking research for work. He'd been told the town's residents wouldn't object to his plans. He hoped that was the case. He'd been here a few days and had spoken to many people. They were so friendly and more than willing to spend a few minutes chatting to him. He'd been made to feel very welcome.

Of course, he hadn't told anyone the real reason why he was there. It was something he'd have to do very soon, and he wasn't looking forward to it. There were always some people who objected to his plans, but once they had the facts and figures, and the reports to confirm his findings, they accepted his proposal.

He sincerely hoped that would happen in this town.

At least being in this new town had taken his mind off his love life. Or lack of love life. He wasn't lucky when it came to love. Lots of his friends were, but never him. He always seemed to pick the wrong woman.

Well, this job would give him a break from all of that. Thank goodness.

He looked more intently towards the shore. He smiled as he saw families sitting on blankets and having picnics. Energetic youngsters threw balls to each other. People were lounging in deckchairs basking in the welcome warmth of the day.

His attention was caught by a movement at the end of the pier. A woman in a long summery dress was flapping her hands around energetically. Her distressed cry carried on the air towards him. What was she so concerned about?

Then he saw a big floppy hat dancing on a gust of wind as it headed his way. Did the hat belong to the woman?

Robin watched the hat as it moved this way and that over the water. It was too far away for him to catch it. He expected it to drop into the sea at any moment. It would be carried further out to sea and beyond, never to be seen again. That was a shame.

The hat suddenly changed direction and came towards his boat. So sudden was the change of direction that Robin just stared at the airborne hat as it swirled around him. It passed within inches of his nose, which caused him to come to his senses. He quickly reached out and grabbed the hat.

He looked towards the woman at the end of the pier. She was watching him. He raised the hat and waved it in the air. She waved back at him and then made some complicated motion with her hands. Robin was too far away to work out what she was trying to convey. He assumed she wanted her hat back. He shook his head at his thoughts. Of course she wanted her hat back!

The shore wasn't that far away. Looking at the woman, he pointed towards it and waved her hat again to make sure she knew what his intentions were.

The woman gave him an energetic nod before turning away and walking along the pier.

Ten minutes later, Robin climbed out of his moored boat with the hat clasped firmly in his hand. He didn't want the wind to whip it free.

The woman was standing on the promenade a short distance from the pier. She was looking at him with a huge smile on her face.

Robin swallowed.

Shoulder-length hair the colour of caramel framed her heart-shaped face. Her light brown eyes were rimmed with a darker brown making them look almost catlike. The sun was shining directly on her, and a ray picked out the dark brown flecks in her eyes. Her smile was mesmerising.

She was so beautiful that she quite took his breath away.

She was saying something and pointing to the hat.

Robin tried to concentrate on her words, but he couldn't. His heart was beating too fast, and his knees felt weak.

She spoke again and then waited for his response.

All Robin could manage was a quiet, "Hi."

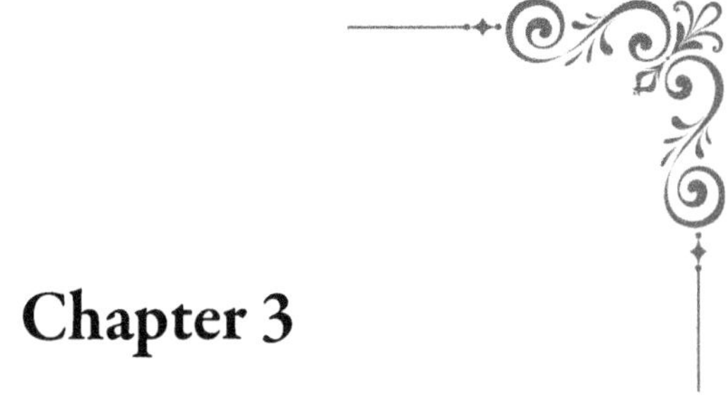

Chapter 3

BECKY

"HI," BECKY SAID.

"Hi," the man repeated, this time with a smile spreading across his face.

And quite a handsome face at that, Becky noted. His tanned skin made his blue eyes sparkle. His dark brown hair flopped casually over to one side. He was wearing jeans and a pale blue shirt with his sleeves rolled up. He seemed to be about her age, perhaps a little older.

"Hi," Becky said for the second time, unable to tear her gaze from his. His smile grew wider. Becky's heart missed a beat, and for a second, she felt as if the earth was tilting beneath her feet. What was happening to her?

The man spoke again. "Hat? Yours?" He held her hat out.

"Yes. Hat. Mine." What was wrong with her? Why couldn't she speak in full sentences?

Still holding the hat towards her, he said, "Hat. My boat. Caught it."

Becky nodded. She took her hat. "Thanks." She couldn't stop looking at him. For some reason, she felt as if they'd known each other all their lives. But how could that be? They'd only just met.

The man blinked, cleared his throat, and said, "Robin. I'm Robin. Robin Hartman." He held his hand out.

"Becky. Becky Carlson. Hi."

They shook hands. Robin's hand was warm and Becky was loath to let go. But she did so.

She cleared her suddenly dry throat and stared intently at the ground. "Thank you for rescuing my hat. I've only had it for two days. I'd been looking at it in the shop for ages. Well, not ages because they've only just got their summer stock in, you know. But since it showed up in the window, I'd been looking at it and thought it was lovely. Just the thing to wear for summer. And I've only had it for two days. Have I already said that? I thought I'd lost it forever." She abruptly stopped talking, aware she was chattering incessantly. She'd gone from one-word sentences to non-stop drivel.

Robin's smile hadn't left his face. "It's a beautiful hat. I thought it was going to fall into the sea. But it didn't."

Becky looked up from the ground. "No, it didn't. You rescued it. Thank you so much." She put the hat on.

Robin's eyes widened. "It really suits you. You look even more—" He stopped talking and swallowed. "It's a nice hat. I'm glad it didn't fall into the sea. Have I already said that?"

"I think so." Becky was back to staring into his eyes.

A noise from her pocket brought her out of her trance. It was her phone. She pulled it out and looked at the message. She sighed.

"Is something wrong?" Robin asked.

"Yes. I was supposed to meet a couple here in an hour, but they've missed their connecting train. There isn't another one until much later on, and they're not sure if they'll get here at all today. That's such a shame. I really wanted to meet then, and I know they were looking forward to coming back here."

"Coming back?"

"Yes. Howard and Joan used to live here years ago. They live in Scotland now."

Robin asked, "Are they coming back for a holiday?"

"They're going to celebrate their fiftieth wedding anniversary. They met here years ago. I haven't got the full story yet, but I know there was a dance at some point. And that's when Howard proposed to Joan."

"Why are you meeting them? If you don't mind me asking?"

"I don't mind at all," Becky replied as she got lost in his blue eyes again. "I work for The Holly Blue Bay Gazette. I'm hoping to write a piece on them. I think our readers will love their story."

Robin smiled. "Who wouldn't like a love story like that?"

"Indeed." Becky tore her eyes away from Robin's and looked back at her phone. "I wonder if there's anything I can do to help."

"Where are they now?"

"At a small train station. It's about sixty miles away. I wish I could pick them up but my car's in the garage." She gave him a wry smile. "It's nearly always in the garage. It spends more time there than it does at my house."

"I can drive you," Robin offered. He pointed along the road. "My car's only over there."

"Oh no! I can't ask you to do that."

"You didn't ask. I offered. I don't mind. I've nothing else to do today."

Becky's common sense came into play. She didn't answer Robin. He was a complete stranger, and he was offering to drive her away from the safety of this town where everyone knew her.

As if reading her thoughts, Robin backed up and held his hands out. "Oh. No. Sorry. I shouldn't have offered. I'm a complete stranger. You shouldn't get into a car with me. I could be a serial killer. Not that I am. But I would say that, wouldn't I? Sorry. Don't listen to me."

"It's okay. It was kind of you to offer." Becky was torn. For some reason, she instinctively trusted Robin, but her sensible side wouldn't let her get into a car with him. She looked at her phone again. She didn't like the idea of Joan and Howard Maxwell being stranded at a train station for hours.

Robin said, "I've got an idea."

Chapter 4

ROBIN

"NO," BECKY SAID AS she shook her head. "No, I can't take your car."

Robin dangled his car keys in front of her. "I insist. It's insured for anyone. There's a full tank of petrol. Go on."

Becky put her hands behind her back. "I can't. I just can't. It's kind of you to offer, but I can't take it."

"What's the alternative? Your couple will be stranded at that station for hours. And what if the next train doesn't turn up? Didn't you say they were in their seventies? You don't want them waiting hours for a train that might not show." He jangled the keys as if trying to hypnotise her.

Becky wavered. "I'm not sure. What will you do? Don't you need your car? What were you going to do this afternoon? What do you do for a job?" She frowned. "Sorry, that's none of my business. It's my nosy reporter side coming out."

Robin shrugged. "I was going to hang around the town this afternoon, that's all. I don't need my car for that."

Becky looked as if she were considering the matter.

At that moment, a regal-looking woman walked by. She nodded at Becky. "Hello, Becky. How are the Gazette's reading figures? Going up, I hope."

"Yes. And for the seventh week in a row," Becky replied. "Roberta, this is Robin Hartman. Erm. He...erm...he's giving me the keys to his car so I can pick someone up."

Robin smiled at the town's mayor. "Hello again. Did you manage to get your front door sorted out?"

"I did," Roberta Wainwright replied. "It's no longer making that dreadful squeaking sound. Why are you lending Becky your car? Can't you take her where she needs to go? Wouldn't that be easier?"

"Yes, it would," Robin said. "But we've only just met, and she quite rightly thinks it's not safe for her to get into a car with a stranger."

"Fair enough, but you're not a stranger to me. I had your background checked out before I asked you to come here. A thorough check." Roberta looked at Becky. "I can vouch for him. You'll be safe if you get in his car. Is it for personal reasons or business?"

"For business reasons. I've got a great feature for the Gazette lined up, and I'm going to interview—"

"No," Roberta interrupted her. "Don't spoil future stories for me. If your visit is for business reasons, then I insist Robin takes you. I assume any petrol costs can be met by the newspaper if needed."

"Yes, they would," Becky admitted.

Roberta pointed to Robin. "Take Becky where she needs to go. Then you can get on with your reports. I'm eager to see what you've discovered. I'll deal with your invoices as soon as I get them."

"Okay," Robin replied quickly. He didn't want to talk about his job any further. He didn't want Becky to know why he was here in Holly Blue Bay. He had a feeling that she wouldn't like it.

Roberta gave them a satisfied smile. "There we are. All sorted out. I'm glad I could help. Goodbye." With that, she walked away.

Becky shook her head at the mayor's departing back but didn't say anything.

Robin suddenly felt awkward. As much as he wanted to spend some time with this lovely woman, he didn't want to force her to do so.

"I don't have to take you. But you can still borrow my car. And don't worry about any petrol costs. It will only mess my accounts up anyway."

Becky gave him a big smile which caused his breath to catch in his throat. To his immense relief, she said, "I'd love to go with you. Can we go now?"

A group of wild horses wouldn't have been able to stop him. "Of course. This way."

Chapter 5

BECKY

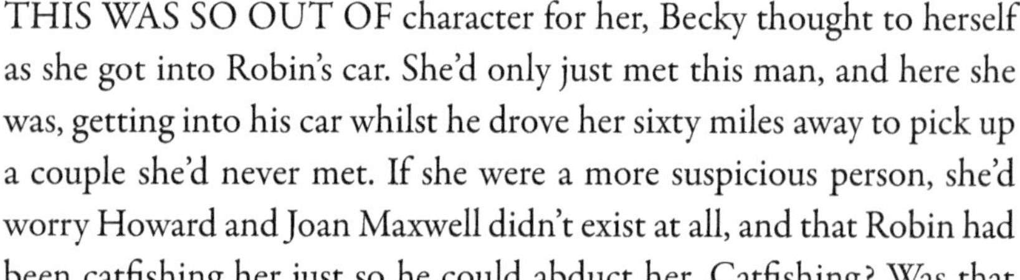

THIS WAS SO OUT OF character for her, Becky thought to herself as she got into Robin's car. She'd only just met this man, and here she was, getting into his car whilst he drove her sixty miles away to pick up a couple she'd never met. If she were a more suspicious person, she'd worry Howard and Joan Maxwell didn't exist at all, and that Robin had been catfishing her just so he could abduct her. Catfishing? Was that the right expression?

But how could he have orchestrated her hat flying off towards his boat which led to them meeting?

No. He wasn't doing that. She was just being silly. She watched too much TV, and her imagination was getting away with her.

But having those ridiculous thoughts was stopping her making sense of her confused feelings. Those feelings which were telling her Robin Hartman was a special man, and they were destined to meet. Every time she glanced at him, her heart felt like it was flipping over. There was a connection between them which she'd never felt with anyone else. Either that, or she'd been out in the sun too long.

Before they set off, Becky sent a text to Joan to say she could pick her and Howard up, if that was okay. Joan's reply was immediate. *'YES PLEASE!!!! THANK YOU!!!!'*

Becky showed Joan's reply to Robin. He smiled warmly, making Becky feel a bit hot and bothered. She gave him the directions and then lowered her window to allow a breeze to cool her warm cheeks.

As they drove out of Holly Blue Bay, nerves made Becky give Robin a running commentary on all the buildings they passed. And the people who lived in them. And the events of their lives which had appeared in the *Gazette*. She couldn't stop talking and started to worry that Robin was going to stop the car and tell her to get out because she was too noisy.

But Robin listened politely, and asked questions now and again which she assumed was either genuine interest or very good manners.

As they left the town behind, Becky's conversation dried up. She had so many questions for Robin, the main one being whether he was single or not. But that wasn't something you could ask a person, was it? She tipped her head to one side as she considered a suitable way of asking him that very question. It could easily come up in conversation. Couldn't it?

The sensible part of her brain decided to make itself known. It asked her why she was so interested. And hadn't she decided not to get involved with anyone again. At least, for the next five years or so.

Whilst she was having a silent argument with herself, she became aware of Robin talking. She gave him her full attention just as he said, "Don't you think so?"

"Pardon? Sorry. I wasn't listening. Could you repeat that?"

Robin smiled. "Am I boring you? One of my ex-girlfriends used to say that I could bore the hind leg off a donkey." He laughed. "That's not even the right expression, but it's one she used over and over again. My less than scintillating conversation is probably why I'm single."

"I'm single too," Becky blurted out. Heat immediately rushed to her face. Why had she said that? "You're not boring, I was thinking about Joan and Howard. Wondering what their story is. What were you talking about whilst I was rudely ignoring you?"

"I was saying how lovely your town is, and how it would make the perfect setting for a romance novel. Everything's so picturesque. I can imagine many people falling in love there."

Becky nodded. "Many people have fallen in love. I've covered most of their stories in the newspaper." She proceeded to tell him about the recent love affairs in the town which included a woman who worked at the library and a man who ran an ice cream stall.

Again, Robin listened politely. He asked appropriate questions, which encouraged Becky to tell him more about the town.

"What about you?" Robin asked. "Tell me more about yourself."

"There's not much to tell. I've always been fascinated with people and their lives. For as long as I can remember, I've read the Gazette. It made the people in my town look like celebrities. I used to cut out my favourite articles and put them in a scrapbook. I've still got those books. And I still read them now and again. What about you? Tell me why you're here."

She didn't know if it was her imagination, but Robin's look became evasive. He said, "I'm a structural engineer, and I'm looking into doing some work for Roberta. I'm staying at the Holly Blue Hotel. Is the music on the radio okay for you? Feel free to change the station. What sort of music do you like?"

They began to chat about other things. The music they liked. Their favourite food and movies. Where they'd been on holiday. Becky was surprised to find they liked a lot of the same things. There were also subjects they didn't agree on, but they disagreed in an easy manner and laughed as they did so.

Within a short time, Becky felt totally at ease in Robin's company. It really was as if they'd known each other for a long time. She felt comfortable with him and almost like she could tell him anything. His evasive manner about his occupation bothered her a little, but maybe he didn't want to bore her with the details of his job.

Time flew by, and before she knew it, they were parking in the railway station where Joan and Howard Maxwell were waiting for her.

It was almost with regret that Becky left the car. She had thoroughly enjoyed being in Robin's company, and selfishly, she didn't want anyone to intrude on that.

She wished it could be just her and him together for the rest of the day.

Why was she feeling like that?

What was this man doing to her?

Chapter 6

HOWARD AND JOAN

JOAN MAXWELL SMILED when she saw the young woman get out of the car. She said to her husband, "Look, that must be Becky. She looks just as I imagined her to. A lovely kind face, and look at how she's smiling at us. Her smile reaches her eyes. I like that in a person. I love that dress she's wearing, it really suits her. I must ask her where she got it from. Howard, do you think a dress like that would suit me?"

Howard replied, "You'd look beautiful in anything. You always do."

Joan gave him a playful push. "You! Let's go and say hello. Isn't it kind of Becky to pick us up? We would have been waiting hours for that next train." She got up from the bench. "And I'm not even certain it would have turned up. We could have been stuck here for an eternity."

"I'd be happy to spend an eternity in your company." Howard stood up, reached for his wife's hand, and kissed the back of it.

Joan laughed. "You're such a charmer."

Howard's eyes crinkled up. "I know. Isn't that why you married me?"

"One of the many reasons." She gently squeezed her husband's hand. She lowered her voice a little. "Who's that handsome chap with Becky? He must be her boyfriend. Look at how he's gazing at her, like he can't believe his luck. And see how Becky's fluttering her eyelashes at him. There's something between them; anyone can see that. They make a lovely couple, don't you think?"

"They might not be a couple."

"If they're not, they should be. I'm always right about these things. You know I am."

"I know you are."

Still holding hands, Howard and Joan walked over to Becky and Robin.

Becky's face lit up. "Mr and Mrs Maxwell?"

"That's us," Joan replied. "But call us Joan and Howard. There's no need to be formal, not after all the emails and texts we've sent each other. I feel as if I already know you, Becky."

Becky's smile grew. "I feel the same. I can't wait to hear the full story of how you two met."

Joan laughed. "I still can't believe you'd be interested in us. We're nothing special."

"But you are," Becky argued. "You were strangers who met in Holly Blue Bay, so that's something special. And didn't you say something about piers? And how important they are to you? I want to know more about that. I love piers, but I am biased because of the beautiful one we have in our town."

Joan noticed Becky's male friend looking away from Becky. It was the first time he'd taken his eyes off her.

Howard said, "We love piers too. It's become our thing, hasn't it, my love? But the one in Holly Blue Bay holds a special place in our hearts." He leaned over and kissed Joan on the cheek.

"Oh, you!" Joan smiled at her husband. She never tired of his kisses. She said to Becky, "Is this your young man?"

Becky's eyes widened. "What? No. No! We've only just met."

"Just met?" Joan repeated.

"Yes. He gave me a lift here."

"What?" Joan's eyebrows rose. "Have you been hitchhiking, Becky? Has this man picked you up from the side of the road? You shouldn't be doing things like that. He could be anyone. Do you even know his name?"

"I do. It's Robin. I don't mean I met him a few minutes ago. And no, I haven't been hitchhiking. I wouldn't do something like that. I've watched enough horror films to know what happens to single women who stand at the side of the road. You see them standing there all vulnerable and usually in something skimpy. Then a car comes along and, well, you know." She stopped talking and pressed her lips together as if trying to stop her next words from tumbling out.

Joan's eyes narrowed a little. Becky was one of those who talked a lot when she was nervous. Why was she nervous? Was it because of Robin? The young man was now back to looking at Becky as if he was under a spell.

Becky explained. "I was standing at the end of the pier in town, and my hat blew off."

Robin took up the tale. "I was in a boat at the time, and I saw the hat coming towards me."

Becky smiled shyly at him. "He caught my hat and then brought it to me."

"Then Becky told me about your predicament," Robin said. "Her car was in the garage, so I offered to drive her here."

"We've had a lovely chat on the way. We've got lots in common." Becky's eyes were twinkling as she gazed at Robin.

"Yeah, we've got lots in common," Robin agreed.

Joan suddenly felt like she was intruding on a private moment. She let out a polite cough which caused the young couple to look away from each other.

Howard pointed to Robin's car and started to say something about the engine. Bless him. He loved talking about cars and could go on about them for hours. She decided to nip the car conversation in the bud, and said, "Robin, it's extremely kind of you to pick us up. Are you ready to take us to Holly Blue Bay? We're excited to see the town again. I hope it hasn't changed that much."

They walked over to Robin's car. He opened the door for Joan which made him go up in her estimation. There weren't many men who did that these days. Then he helped Howard put their luggage in the boot of the car. She smiled to herself when she heard Howard talking about cars again. He just couldn't help himself.

Within minutes, they were driving away from the railway station. Howard took his wife's hand once more, and they shared a loving look.

As they drove along, Joan couldn't help but notice a similar kind of look passing between Becky and Robin. They were obviously attracted to each other, but she had a strange feeling that things were not going to run smoothly for them.

Chapter 7

ROBIN

ROBIN DROVE THE COUPLE to the hotel. It was the same one he was staying at. He insisted on taking Howard and Joan's luggage inside. There were only a couple of bags and it was no trouble for him. As they entered the hotel, Howard started to talk about cars again which Robin appreciated because it took his mind off Becky.

He couldn't stop thinking about how Becky had answered Joan's question about him being her young man. Becky had been so adamant that he wasn't. Was it such a horrific thought? He couldn't work out if she liked him or not. She'd seemed very interested in the things he'd talked about on their journey. But was she just being polite?

He knew how he felt about her. He didn't know he could feel so strongly about a woman he'd met a few hours ago. He couldn't stop thinking about how their eyes had locked when they'd first seen each other. And how he was so tongue-tied that he couldn't produce more than a feeble, 'Hi.' He'd heard about people falling in love at first sight, but that happened to other people.

Didn't it?

His emotions were all over the place. One thing he was sure of was that he liked Becky. He liked her a lot. And he wanted to spend more time with her.

There was one thing which was bothering him. The situation over the pier.

But there was nothing he could do about that.

Chapter 8

BECKY

BECKY COULDN'T STOP looking at Joan and Howard Maxwell as they checked into the hotel. They kept looking at each and smiling. It was like they were the only people in the world. She loved how Howard kept kissing his wife, and how they held hands whenever possible. It made Becky's heart want to sing for joy at the sight of them. Not that her heart could sing, she reasoned, but if it could she was certain it would sing a joyful tune.

Robin was still carrying the suitcases. Howard had tried to take them back, but Robin said it was no trouble for him to carry them. It was kind of him to do that.

Becky waited until the couple were checked in, then she went over to them and said, "When would you like the interview to go ahead? Well, it's not an interview really. I don't know why I call it that. It's more of a conversation. A chat, I suppose."

Joan placed her hand on Becky's arm. "I know what you mean. I'd love to talk soon, but me and my Howard need to get settled in the hotel first. Then I'm going to need a strong cup of tea!"

"Oh, of course," Becky said. "Sorry. I'm being a nuisance. I didn't mean to rush you. I'm very eager to hear your story. We can always do it tomorrow. You've got my number. I'm free all day."

"We can do it today," Joan insisted. "I want to talk to you, not only about me and Howard, but about you."

"Me? Why?"

"Because you're interesting, and so are the stories you've written. I want to know all about you, and how long you've been working at the Gazette. Howard and I still read it. We read it online now. Thank goodness for the internet. We don't know most of the people in the reports, but sometimes we do. We both miss the town. Me more than him, but I can't complain about where we've set up home. Scotland is a marvellous place to live."

Becky said, "I can't imagine living anywhere other than this town."

Joan smiled. "That's what I used to think until I met Howard. Then I would have travelled to the ends of the earth just to be with him. Love does that to you. You know that. You must have been in love."

"I'm not sure I ever have."

Joan glanced at Robin. "You never know when love is going to strike. Why don't you join us for something to eat? I'm famished. I only brought a couple of sandwiches for our journey, and we ate them within an hour of setting off. Do they still do sausage and mash in the restaurant here?"

"They do."

"Smashing. I could just eat that, and I know my Howard would love it. Why don't you wait in the dining room for us? Give us ten minutes, then we'll join you." She gently squeezed Becky's arm. "Thanks so much for picking us up. You're an angel." She returned to Howard's side and gave him that loving look again.

Robin still had the suitcases in his hands. He looked Becky's way, gave her a nod and a brief smile and then followed the couple up the stairs .

Becky felt a pang of sadness as she watched Robin walking away. She didn't want him to go. She didn't know much about his job, or how long he was staying in the town. She had no idea what he was going to do with the rest of the day. She should have taken his number. But then what? She wasn't brave enough to phone him.

She wondered if she would ever see him again.

Her steps were heavy as she headed to the dining room. It was weird to feel so strongly about someone so soon. What was going on with her?

She spoke to the waitress in the dining room and was led over to a table which looked out over the bay. The magnificent view usually raised Becky's spirits. But it didn't today.

She was staring so morosely out of the window that she didn't notice someone sitting down opposite her.

She only noticed him when he said, "Hi."

Chapter 9

ROBIN

"HI," BECKY SAID TO him with a growing smile on her face.

"Hi," Robin repeated. What was wrong with him? Why had he gone back to one-word sentences? But look at her eyes. He felt like he was getting lost in them. Such an unusual shade of brown. What did that colour remind of him of? Caramel? Maybe. Coffee? No, too light. Copper? Perhaps the burnished copper of a treasured item.

His wandering thoughts were interrupted by Becky. "Robin? Are you okay?"

"I'm fine, just fine. Are you okay?"

She smiled some more. "Yes. I asked if you were staying for something to eat?"

"I am. Joan insisted. She said she and Howard wanted to repay my kindness by buying me lunch. I told them there was no need, but Joan was firm about it. I didn't feel I could argue with her."

Becky laughed. "Yes, she does have that way about her. Don't you have work to do?"

"Are you trying to get rid of me?"

"No! Not at all." She picked up her napkin and began to fiddle with it. "I was hoping to see you again. I didn't say thank you for coming to my assistance. Not just with my hat, but with picking Joan and Howard up. You are kind."

Robin made a weird sort of *pfft* noise which didn't sound at all masculine. He cleared his throat, and said, "It was nothing. Anyone would have done that."

"They wouldn't." She continued to smile.

He smiled right back.

His smile vanished when she asked, "What work are you doing here? You haven't given me the full details. You said you're an engineer. Are you doing some building work in the town?"

Robin shifted in his seat. "Not really. I don't want to bore you with the details."

"You won't bore me."

"I would. What's good to eat here?" He picked a menu up and focused on it. He'd already eaten a few times in this restaurant, and he knew the food was excellent. But talking about food meant he didn't have to discuss his work.

They spent the next ten minutes talking about the various dishes on the menu. Then Robin pointed towards the spectacular view of the bay and asked Becky to tell him more about the town.

As she was doing that, Robin allowed his mind to return to appreciative thoughts about Becky. There was a lot to admire. Even though he'd sworn off love, he wanted to get to know Becky more. He wanted to know everything about her. Everything.

Could he ask her out on a date? Would she say yes?

Realising his mind had wandered off again, he forced himself to concentrate on what Becky was saying.

She said, "Of all the lovely areas in this town, the pier is my very favourite. I've always loved it. Mum said I took my first steps on there! Whenever I'm feeling down, I know a stroll along the pier will make me feel happy. Even when it's raining. There's something magical about it. It's my favourite place in the world."

Disappointment ran through Robin. He couldn't ask Becky out. Not ever.

Chapter 10

BECKY

BECKY STOPPED TALKING about the pier because a strange look appeared on Robin's face. She couldn't work out what the look meant. Was she boring him by going on about the pier all the time? Or had there been a terrible experience in his past concerning a pier? A family tragedy? Whatever it was, she didn't want to increase his discomfort. She made a mental note to stop talking about the pier so much.

But that didn't last long because Joan and Howard walked into the dining room. Becky noticed how they were holding hands again. Howard's glance kept going left and right as they walked along as if sussing out the area and making sure there weren't any hidden dangers which could hurt his beloved wife. Becky wasn't sure what those dangers could be. A stray chair which hadn't been pushed under a table far enough? Something which had been dropped on the floor and could prove a tripping hazard? Becky loved the way Howard looked out for his wife. It made her wistful for her future husband.

If there ever was one.

The happy couple approached the table and sat down on either side of Becky.

Joan said, "I hope you haven't been waiting too long for us. We got chatting in our room. Seeing this town again brought back so many happy memories. Have you ordered yet?"

"Not yet," Becky spoke for both her and Robin. "I'm ready to order now, though. Robin?"

Robin was staring at the menu as if he'd never seen one before. "I haven't got much of an appetite." He pushed the menu to one side. "I should get back to work."

"Nonsense," Joan's reply came quickly. "If you don't want any food, you could still stay for a cup of tea. No one can say no to a cup of tea. Howard, what are you having?"

Howard chuckled. "As if you need to ask. Sausage and mash for me." He looked at Becky. "It was the first meal we shared back in the day. And it was in this hotel. But not at this table. It was that one in the corner. The weather has just turned nasty, and the rain was fair coming down. But we didn't mind, did we." He gazed at Joan.

"We didn't." She patted Howard's hand. "Let's not get all slushy when people are about to eat." She gave the waitress a friendly wave to beckon her over.

Becky decided to have the same as Joan and Howard. She'd never had sausage and mash here, and it sounded delicious. Robin didn't order any food, but at Joan's insistence, he did ask for a cup of tea. Becky wondered if he was desperate to get away from them all. Or was it just her? Was he regretting rescuing her hat now? If he hadn't, he could be getting on with his engineering work instead. Whatever that entailed.

Whilst they waited for the food to arrive, Becky asked Joan to tell them more about her and Howard. She especially wanted to know how they ended up dancing on the pier. Robin winced slightly at Becky's question which made her surmise something terrible must have happened in Robin's past if even the mention of a pier brought out such uncomfortable emotions.

Joan clasped her hands together. "There was a special dance that evening. A celebration. Something to do with the town's history. It was a lovely summer's evening. There had been rain earlier in the day, and we worried the dance wouldn't go ahead. But then, like magic, the skies cleared in the afternoon and the sun appeared. As the night came along, the stars seemed brighter than ever as if they'd been washed by the day's rain. There was a full moon too."

"I saw a shooting star," Howard said.

"Oh, yes. I remember that." Joan reached out and touched Howard's hand. Becky wondered if she should change places so that they could be closer to each other. But that would mean her sitting next to Robin, and she didn't think he wanted that.

Joan continued. "It was an enchanted evening, in my mind anyway. It became even more magical when Howard asked me to dance. As soon as I was in his arms, an immense feeling of peace and security went through me. It was like I'd come home, do you know what I mean?"

Becky nodded even though she'd never experienced anything like that with a person. With her house, yes, but not with a person. What must that feel like?

"I felt the same," Howard added. "It was like I'd been waiting for that moment all my life. I didn't want to let you go. I could have danced all night."

Joan laughed. "I think we did dance all night. Or at least until the band stopped playing. I didn't think things could get more magical, but then you proposed. I actually felt like I was flying."

Becky put her elbows on the table and rested her chin on her hands. "Howard, did you know you were going to propose?"

"No. Not after all that had gone on between me and Joan before that pier dance. I wasn't even sure we were going to ever talk to each other again. Not after all the arguments we'd had. I thought Joan hated me."

There was a sudden silence.

Becky said, "Pardon? What do you mean? I thought you were in love."

Joan took her hand away from her husband's and folded her arms. "Howard, I thought we agreed not to talk about that. It's all in the past."

"But I was answering Becky's question."

"She doesn't need to know what went on before our pier dance."

Becky said, "I'd like to know."

"I don't like talking about it," Joan said firmly. She looked towards the kitchen. "How long does it take to cook sausage and mash? We've been waiting ages."

In a gentler tone, Howard said, "Joan, love, it's okay to talk about our past. It's all part of our history. Without that part, we wouldn't be where we are now."

"I know that, but talking about it makes me so angry. And sad. All that time we wasted being angry with each other. I don't like to think about it." She blinked quickly, and Becky was distressed to see tears in her eyes.

Howard must have seen them too because he stood up and went around to his wife. He hugged her and murmured, "It's okay. We won't talk about it."

She gave him a grateful smile. He returned to his seat and everything seemed fine again. But Becky couldn't help wondering what had gone on between them. Would they ever tell her? She certainly wasn't going to raise the subject again, not going by the effect it had on Joan.

Joan expertly changed the subject and began to talk about many other things including Becky's career and the stories she'd covered. Even when the food arrived, Joan managed to keep up a stream of questions. She kept away from the topic of her early relationship with Howard.

Robin listened closely when Becky spoke about the various incidents she'd written about. He seemed interested in the town and the people who lived here. At one point he said, "For a small town, there's a lot going on."

Joan smiled at his words. "There's never a dull moment in this town. It's the people who make a town, don't you think?"

Becky nodded. "And the buildings too. Especially all the beautiful ones we have here."

They chatted some more as they finished their food. Robin hadn't changed his mind about ordering something to eat, but he did seem to be enjoying his tea.

Once the meal was finished, Howard stood up and patted his stomach. "I need to walk some of this off. Joan, my love, would you care to take a stroll around this delightful town with me? I might even buy you an ice cream later."

"How can I resist such an offer?" Joan replied with a smile. She looked at Becky. "I haven't given you much information about me and Howard. It's not much to write a story about."

Becky's reporter instinct knew there was much more to Joan and Howard's story, but she would have to dig carefully to uncover it. "Why don't we meet up again tomorrow? We can meet on the pier, and I can take some photos."

"We can meet tomorrow," Joan said, "but not on the pier. We're not going on it until it's the day of our anniversary. Isn't that right, Howard?"

"It certainly is. Only three days to go until we recreate that magical moment which changed my life for the better."

Joan linked her arm through his. "You say the sweetest things. No wonder I love you so much. Becky, let me know when and where tomorrow, and we'll be there. Why don't you show Robin around the town this afternoon?"

Becky looked away from Robin. "I'm sure he's already had a look around."

"Maybe," Joan said, "but not from a resident's point of view. You know a lot about the town and its secrets. I'm sure Robin would like to spend a few hours with you."

Becky wasn't sure about that at all. Robin looked like he wanted to run out of the room. She gave him a direct look, and said, "Well? Do you want me to show you around the town?"

Chapter 11

ROBIN

ROBIN DIDN'T KNOW WHAT to say. He had work to do, but he wanted to spend time with Becky. He decided his work could wait.

With a smile on his face, he said, "I would love that. Let me settle the bill and then we can go."

"No way!" Howard almost exploded. "The bill is going on our hotel account, lad. This is our way of saying thank you. And you've only had a cup of tea so there's no way we'd expect you to pay for everything."

"But—" Robin attempted to argue.

Howard waved his objections away. Then he took Joan by the hand and they left the room. Robin saw how close they walked. It was clear they were deeply in love. And after all those years together. What must that feel like?

Becky said to him, "Have you seen the church? St Agatha's? It's just across the way. If we're lucky, we might get to speak to Reverend Pendleton. He's quite a character."

"I haven't seen the church," Robin admitted. "Do you know old it is? And what style it's built in?"

"I don't, but I'm sure the reverend will."

"Sorry for the questions. It's the engineer in me, I love looking at buildings."

"It's good to feel passionate about something." Her look lingered a bit too long. "Let's go."

They left the hotel and walked the short distance to the church.

Becky explained, "There's been a lot of work on the church lately, especially the roof. You won't have met Daisy Clarke because she's on her honeymoon at the moment. She came to the town last year to improve the tourist trade. She held lots of events and raised funds to get the roof fixed. She met her husband Jacob, here last year. I told you about them earlier."

"I remember." Robin looked at the church they were approaching. Becky was walking very close to him, and he could smell her floral perfume. There was a hint of rose in it. He tried to take his mind off how lovely she smelled by concentrating on the church. His attention went to the roof. It did look in good repair. And those arched windows were beautiful.

"Oops!" Becky stumbled on the path and bumped into him.

Robin put his hand on her arm to steady her. All thoughts of the church fled from his mind. "Are you okay?"

"Yes." She looked behind her. "I don't even know what I tripped over. Sorry about that."

"No problem." Robin reluctantly took his hand away.

They continued along the path and into the church. Robin took a moment to appreciate the internal structure. It really was a magnificent building.

Becky said, "There have been a lot of weddings here, and other events. There was a time when not many people came here, but that changed after Daisy arrived and got to work."

"She's an angel," a man in a black cassock said as he seemingly appeared out of thin air. "I bless the day when she appeared in our lives. She's performed miracles." He aimed his next words at Robin. "I'm Reverend Enoch Pendleton. It's always a pleasure to have a new face in the church. Haven't I seen you around the town? And I believe you're staying at the hotel."

Robin's eyebrows shot up. "That's right."

Reverend Pendleton laughed. "Don't look so surprised. I get around. I see things. It keeps my parishioners on their toes because they never know when I'm right behind them in the streets. I'm like a dark spectre sometimes, hiding in the shadows. According to my sources, you are Robin Hartman."

"That's right." Robin became wary. What was the reverend going to say next? Hopefully nothing about why he was in town. He quickly took control of the conversation. "This is a beautiful church. Can you tell me more about it?"

The reverend's face lit up. "People never ask me that! I have many, many interesting facts about this building. Follow me, young man, and we'll start in the oldest part of the church. I hope you're not squeamish; there are some very dark stories linked to this intriguing building."

Becky's face lit up. "I didn't know that. Tell us more."

Robin laughed at her eager expression.

She blushed a little, and said, "I do love a bit of horror. I like being scared. I watch a lot of horror movies. I love them."

"I'm just the opposite," Robin admitted. "But I don't mind a scary story."

Becky joked, "If you get too scared, you can hold my hand."

Robin was tempted to take her hand right now. "I might take you up on that offer."

Becky blushed some more before following Reverend Pendleton down the aisle.

As interesting as the reverend's talk was, Robin couldn't stop thinking about Becky. Perhaps he should tell her what he was doing in the town. Perhaps she would understand.

And maybe she wouldn't. Once she knew the truth about him, she wouldn't want anything to do with him. She wouldn't talk to him, and she might even start to hate him. The thought of that sent waves of sadness rushing through him. Why did he care so much about what she thought about him?

Reverend Pendleton was saying something about some underground tunnels which led from the church to the beach. "The tunnels have only been discovered recently by one of our locals, Maureen Davenport. She used to work at the library but she's gone off on some of her travels with her chap. What's his name again, Becky?"

"Cliff," Becky replied. She said to Robin, "I told you about Maureen and Cliff."

A chuckle came from the reverend. "I think there's magic in the air. Lots of couples get together, even those who don't seem matched at first. But isn't that always the case? The path of true love seldom runs smoothly. Not in this town, anyway. But if people are meant to be together, then love finds a way."

Robin shared a quick look with Becky. He wasn't sure love would find a way with them. Unless he did something about it. A certainty came over him. He had to tell her the truth and deal with whatever she said.

The reverend was talking again. "Robin, if you have time later, you can venture into the tunnels. They're quite safe. Unless you're claustrophobic. We've had a few incidents of people panicking when they've been underground. But I'm sure Becky will look after you. She's been in the tunnels many times."

"I'll keep you safe," Becky said with a smile. "We can go there now, if you want to?"

"I'm not sure," Robin replied. It wasn't that he was scared to go into the tunnels, well, not much. But he didn't want to tell Becky the truth about himself when they were in a confined space. There was a chance she would storm off in anger, and he didn't want that. He also didn't want to be left alone in unfamiliar tunnels. But there again, maybe he deserved to left alone underground. He should have told her the truth as soon as they'd met. Then she would have taken her hat back and walked away in disgust. And then he would never have fallen for her.

The truth hit him like a brick.

He had fallen for her.

Big time.

Robin lightly touched Becky on the arm. "I need to tell you something."

"Now?" she asked.

"Yes, now."

As if sensing the urgency in Robin's voice, Reverend Pendleton looked at his wrist, and said, "Is that the time? Goodness me! Doesn't time fly sometimes? I shall have to cut our tour short. I have somewhere very important to be. It was lovely to meet you, Robin. If you'd like to resume our tour, do get in touch. I must fly! Cheerio."

With that, he briskly walked away from them and through a side door.

Robin said, "Can we go somewhere else to talk? Maybe somewhere private?"

Becky frowned. "Is it going to be a difficult conversation?"

He nodded.

"In that case, we'll go to the pier. Difficult conversations always seem easier there. The pier seems to make problems disappear. Come on." She walked away from him.

Robin let out a groan. The pier was the last place he wanted to be.

Chapter 12

BECKY

As soon as Becky woke up the next morning, her thoughts went to Robin. That was a weird conversation they'd had at the church yesterday. Or rather, it was going to be the start of a weird conversation but they didn't get very far with it. As soon as they'd left the church, Robin had received a phone call. He'd sounded annoyed at whoever was calling and had tried to put them off, but he hadn't been successful. He'd apologised profusely to her, and said he had to go. He promised to phone her later. They'd exchanged numbers, but he hadn't called.

And that had annoyed Becky. She'd spent too many hours waiting for men to text or phone her. She wasn't going to put up with it from anyone else, certainly not a man she barely knew.

Her thoughts immediately betrayed her, and a soft smile came to her face as she recalled the time they'd spent together yesterday. Robin was lovely. He was kind and thoughtful. And considerate. And very handsome. Those eyes of his...

She pulled a face. Nice eyes or not, he hadn't phoned. And she wasn't going to wait around for him. If he had something to say, then he could find her and tell her face to face. She had other things to do than wait around for a man. She was intrigued about what he'd wanted to talk about, but she had a life to live.

She quickly showered and got dressed. After a quick breakfast, she headed to the hotel to meet Joan and Howard. Joan had sent her a message last night asking if Becky could join them at the hotel. They wanted to talk about their relationship in more detail, and Joan had some old photos which she wanted to show Becky. Some were of the pier and would make excellent images for her piece in the paper. She didn't know whether she wanted Joan to talk about the turbulent time before Howard had proposed to her. From a professional point of view, it could make her article more interesting. But from a personal perspective, she didn't want Joan to get upset again.

Becky found the couple in the lounge area of the hotel. They were snuggled next to each other on a corner sofa. Howard was whispering something in Joan's ear, and Joan was giggling which made her look years younger. As soon as they saw Becky approaching Joan gave Howard and gentle shove and told him to behave.

Joan smiled at Becky. "Good morning. It's lovely to see you again. I do love your dress. That colour brings out the brown of your lovely eyes. Has anyone told you you've got lovely eyes?"

"Not recently, but thank you for the compliment," Becky said. "How was your evening? Did you enjoy strolling around the town? Has it changed much since you were last here?"

Joan indicated for Becky to take a seat opposite them. "We had a super time. The memories came flooding back. The town looks mainly the same, which I'm pleased about. There are some of those coffee shops and fast-food places which seem to be in every town these days, but what can you do? You have to move with the times. But the magic of the town is still here." She stopped talking and shared a look with Howard. He gave her a slight nod as if knowing what she was going to say next. She continued, "We're thinking about coming back here to live."

"Really?" Becky said. "That would be wonderful. What part of town would you live in?"

"Somewhere with a sea view," Joan said. "I love looking at the sea, it's so relaxing. Where do you live?"

"Halfway up the main hill. I've got a view of the pier. I never tire of looking at it. It's my favourite part of town. If I could live on it, then I would." Becky smiled. "It'd be wonderful to have a little house right at the end of the pier. It would be a dream come true. For me, anyway."

Howard took a sharp intake of breath and looked as if he were going to say something. Joan noticed, and gave him a firm look. His eyebrows rose in question. Joan's look turned more severe.

Becky asked, "Is there something wrong?"

"No. Nothing," Joan said. "There's nothing wrong. We were tempted to go on the pier, but we're going to wait until it's our anniversary. Speaking of which, are you ready for the full details of how we met? I'm warning you now that it's not that interesting."

Becky took her phone from her bag. "Would you mind if I recorded it? I won't publish the story until you've had a look at what I've written."

"I don't mind if your record us. I hope my voice comes across okay." Joan folded her hands on her lap. "Ready?"

Becky set her phone to record. "Ready."

Joan began to tell Becky about how she'd first set eyes on Howard Maxwell all those years ago. "Our eyes met across a crowded room. It didn't take us long to get together. We had a bit of a fallout at one point, but things worked themselves out. And now, here we are, happily married."

Becky frowned. She wasn't getting the full story here. "Can you give me more details? Where did you first see him?"

"At a dance. There used to be a dance every week at the church hall. We were both twenty-four at the time. That seems centuries ago! I can't believe we used to be that young."

Howard put his arm around his wife's shoulders. "You've barely aged a day."

"You!" Joan let out a tinkle of a laugh. "You say the sweetest things."

"I mean it."

Joan went on, "As soon as I locked eyes with Howard, I felt a jolt of electricity running through me. I thought I was having a funny turn at first. I couldn't tear my eyes away from him. It was like he was looking into my soul. Have you ever experienced that with anyone, Becky?"

"No," Becky lied.

"I hope you do one day. Even after all these years, I keep thinking about that moment," Joan said. "When we looked at each other that first time, it was like we'd known each other for years, or even from another life."

Howard interjected, "It was like our souls recognised each other, and now that we'd met, there was no going back."

Joan nodded. "He moved towards me, and I stood there gazing at him, wondering what on earth was happening to me. And then he spoke."

Howard chuckled. "I could only manage one word. Her beauty knocked the breath right out of me. I could only manage a hello."

"And I said hello back. My words had deserted me too," Joan admitted. "And that wasn't like me at all."

Howard's face was full of tenderness. "We said hello a few more times and just smiled at each other like a couple of love-struck fools. We were under a spell."

Becky looked down at her phone. She had experienced the very same thing yesterday with Robin, but she wasn't going to share that with Joan and Howard. The fact that he hadn't phoned her confirmed he hadn't felt the same thing. Why was she such a fool when it came to love? When would she ever learn?

"Is something wrong?" Joan asked. "You look really sad."

Becky forced a smile to her face. "Nothing's wrong. What happened after you met?"

"Howard asked me to dance, and we were inseparable for the rest of the night."

"She was so light on her feet," Howard said. "Like a feather floating across the dance floor. I could have danced all night, just like in that famous song."

Joan sat upright. "Oh! Dancing! I nearly forgot. Becky, we've arranged for a little dance session at the church hall. Some of our friends are going to be there. The dances will be things like the waltz and foxtrot, that sort of thing. We'd love for you to join us."

Becky shook her head. "Oh no. I can't dance. Not dances like those. I could come along and watch, maybe take some photos. When is it?"

Joan stood up. "In ten minutes. It completely slipped my mind. We should have been there a few minutes ago to welcome our guests. Howard, come on. Becky, we'll see you there soon. I'm sure there'll be someone who can give you a dance lesson. There's nothing quite like having a handsome man hold you gently in his arms as you move around the room. See you soon!"

"What about the rest of your story?" Becky called after them.

Joan didn't answer as she rushed out of the room with Howard.

Becky stared after them. This story was taking much longer to write than she'd anticipated. She made a few notes on her phone before putting it away. Then she left the hotel and headed to the church hall. She had meant to casually ask Joan if she'd seen Robin in the hotel today. She was glad she hadn't. She needed to put all thoughts of that man out of her head.

Chapter 13

HOWARD AND JOAN

"WHAT ARE YOU UP TO now, my love?" Howard asked his wife as they walked towards the church hall.

"Just giving love a helping hand, that's all. You saw how miserable Robin looked when he came back to the hotel last night. Something's going on with his business. I heard on the grapevine he's doing some work on behalf of the council. And he's been having meetings with Roberta Wainwright."

"Who's she again?" Howard put his hand on Joan's arm to steady her as she walked along the path.

"She's the mayor. I haven't met her yet, but I've been told she's very stern when it comes to council matters. She's one for cutting the budgets wherever she can. I can only imagine what she's asked Robin to do. Well, I told you last night, didn't I? You saw how his face dropped when Becky started talking about the pier. It wouldn't surprise me if the mayor thought something needed to be done about it."

Howard sighed heavily. "I know. It is an old structure, though. It's not going to last forever. I noticed how much it was leaning to one side. You saw it too. I was about to tell Becky about it."

Joan stopped in her tracks. "I know you were! That's why I stopped you. Don't write that pier off just yet. You know what happened to it years ago. And how things turned out."

"How will I ever forget that?" He leaned over and kissed her on the cheek. "I felt sorry for Becky when she said she'd love a little house on the pier. That's never going to happen, poor lass."

Joan continued walking. "Everyone's got to have a dream. I can't help her with her pier dream, but I can help her with the other one."

"Which other one?"

Joan smiled at her husband. "The one about Robin. You saw how they looked at each other yesterday. But something's gone wrong between them, I can sense it. They need to talk. They need to be together."

"Can't you leave them to sort things out on their own?"

"No. We're only here for a little while. I can't go back to Scotland if they haven't sorted things out. They can't repeat our mistakes. You don't want that for them, do you?"

"I wouldn't wish that on anyone. What's your big plan, then?"

They stopped at the doors of the hall. "I'll need to speak to the reverend first. I hope he's in." Joan told him what her plan was.

Howard shook his head. "They'll never fall for that."

Chapter 14

ROBIN

Robin frowned as he rushed towards the church hall. He hoped this wouldn't take too long. He had lots of things he needed to get done today. He didn't know why she wanted to see him here of all places. It was lucky that he was so nearby.

As he got nearer the doors, he heard the sound of old-fashioned music inside. What was going on in there? Some sort of dance?

He entered the hall and came to an abrupt stop.

"There you are!" Joan called over to him. "I've been waiting for you. I'm in desperate need of a dancing partner. As you can see, Becky is dancing with my husband and I've been left all alone."

Robin caught Becky's eye as she was twirled smoothly around the floor. There was a look of panic on her face. He had to stop himself from rushing over and rescuing her. All of a sudden, her expression changed and she started to laugh. Hearing that sound made his heart feel lighter.

Joan walked over to Robin and took his hands in hers. "Do you know how to waltz?"

"No. Your text said you wanted to give me some money for petrol. You don't have to do that. By the way, how did you get my number?"

"How about the tango? You must be able to do that?"

"No. Did Becky give you my number?"

"Salsa? That's not too difficult. Come with me."

"Joan, just a minute." Robin felt himself being moved across the floor. Joan was much stronger than she looked. "I only came here in answer to your text. I'd just returned to the hotel when I got it."

"Did you? That's a coincidence." Joan's eyes were wide with innocence. "You didn't have to call in."

"But your text said you wanted to see me urgently. In person."

"Did it? It's just an expression. You could have sent a reply text. But I'm glad you're here now."

"The petrol money," Robin began, "there's no need for it."

He expected Joan to argue, but she surprised him by saying, "Okay. Fair enough. You're here now, so you might as well have a dance. I'll show you the steps. Put one hand here, and the other here." She manhandled him until they were in a position similar to Howard and Becky. Then in a series of twists and turns, she moved them across the wooden floor until they were just feet away from her husband and his captive partner.

Robin shot a "what's happening?" look at Becky. She shrugged helplessly in reply. Robin attempted to tell Joan several times that he didn't have time for dancing, but she expertly ignored him.

Joan proceeded to give Robin a series of instructions which seemed incredibly complicated to begin with, but after a while, Robin picked up the pattern in them and stopped standing on Joan's feet so much.

"I think you're getting the hang of it," Joan told him a few dances later. "Let's have one more dance and then you'll be ready."

"Ready? Ready for what?"

"You'll see."

They had one more dance. Robin became confident in his steps and found himself actually enjoying the movements. He kept looking at Becky who seemed to be enjoying the dancing as much as he was.

Joan manoeuvred him over to Howard and Becky just as the music stopped. She swiftly released Robin, and said, "Time to change partners." She gently pushed him towards Becky who was, coincidently, freed from Howard's arms at that very moment. Her momentum caused her to bump into Robin.

"Oh, I'm so sorry," Becky said.

"No, that's fine. My fault," Robin murmured.

"No, no. It's mine." Becky gave him a bashful look.

Joan cried out, "Less talking. More dancing."

"Do you want to dance?" Robin asked Becky.

"I don't think we have a choice," she replied with a small smile.

"We don't have to. We can leave." Robin looked into her eyes and thought, *please don't go, please don't go.*

Becky said, "I suppose we can stay for one dance. I think I've got the hang of it."

"Me too. I apologise now if I stand on your feet."

She laughed. "The same goes for me."

He gently put one hand on her shoulder and placed his other in her outstretched palm. He pulled her a little bit closer. His heart thundered in his chest at having her so near. This felt so right. He was tempted to pull her even closer but restrained himself from doing so.

The next tune began. Robin and Becky began to move around the floor. Uncertainly at first, but their confidence soon grew along with their smiles.

Robin asked Becky, "How did you end up here?"

"They tricked me. Joan said there was going to be a group of their friends here for a dance. She more or less insisted that I come along as well. When I got here, there was only her and Howard here. Joan said their friends couldn't make it."

Robin smiled. "All of them?"

Becky laughed. "Yes, all of them. What are you doing here?"

"I was bamboozled just like you. Joan said she wanted to see me in person as soon as possible to give me some money for petrol." He softly looked into her eyes. "I'm glad she tricked me."

Becky held his gaze. "I'm glad she tricked both of us."

They didn't talk for the next two dances.

When the last song ended, Robin took a step back from Becky. "I'm sorry I didn't phone you back. I was going to, but I wanted to talk to you in person instead. There's something I should have told you yesterday. Something important."

"Okay. I'm listening."

Chapter 15

BECKY

Becky unconsciously held her breath whilst she waited for Robin to speak. Going by the serious look in his eyes, she wasn't entirely sure she wanted to hear his words.

Robin looked over at Joan and Howard who were still dancing. He lowered his voice a little as he said, "Perhaps we should go somewhere else. Somewhere more private."

"The pier? It's not usually busy at this time of the day."

He shook his head. "Not the pier."

Becky didn't get the chance to think of a suitable place to go because Joan came over to them and said, "Are you two ready for a rest? Becky, I'd like to tell you more about Howard and me. I haven't told you about our pier adventures yet. Howard's just politely told me I've taken up too much of your time, and that I should let you know our story. Then you can get on with any other articles you're waiting to write."

Becky did want to know more about Joan and Howard, but she also wanted to know what Robin was going to say.

Robin made the decision for her. "I'd like to hear about your pier adventures, Joan. I'm intrigued."

Becky and Robin followed Joan to the other side of the room where Howard was sitting at a table which had four chairs arranged around it. From somewhere, he had produced a jug of water and some glasses. He poured some water for everyone.

Once they'd had a refreshing drink, and Becky had set her phone to record, Joan began to talk. "Becky, I'm like you when it comes to the pier here in town. I love it, and all the shops on it. There's nothing quite like standing at the end of it on a clear day and staring out to sea. It makes your heart feel good."

Becky nodded in agreement.

Joan continued, "The pier became more magical for me after Howard proposed on it. Because of his job, we left the town soon later and moved around the country. I hated leaving Holly Blue Bay, but I would have followed Howard anywhere."

Howard said, "She missed seeing the pier every day. I felt bad for taking her away, but I had to travel with my job. I hated seeing my Joan so sad, so I had to do something."

Joan took up the tale. "Whenever we were near a town or city which had a pier, my lovely Howard would make sure we spent some time on it." She smiled over at him. "He always brought some music with him when we went on those piers. It was the music which we first danced to in this very hall. Even if there wasn't much space on the pier, or if it was crowded, we would always have a dance no matter what. I was a bit embarrassed at first, but once I was in Howard's arms, I didn't care about people watching us."

Becky smiled as she imagined the couple heading out onto a busy pier and starting to dance. "I bet people loved seeing you. Did anyone ever join in with the dancing?"

"They did!" Joan said. "Not all the time. Sometimes, they looked at us as if we were mad. But often, they would join in. It was lovely. We've got some great memories of our dances."

"And the piers we went to," Howard added. "Did you know, there are over fifty piers in England and Wales."

Robin said, "Yes, I did know."

Becky shot him a curious look. Why did he know that?

"Blackpool is one of my favourites," Joan said. "There's more than one pier there, but I love the central one with its big wheel and fairground. I don't think anyone is ever too old for a fairground."

Howard laughed at her words. "We always go on the rides when we're there. I really like Cromer Pier. It's got a theatre on it. We've been to a few shows there on an evening. Then we have a couple of drinks before waltzing around the pier. We've been lucky with the weather every time we've been. We've never been caught in the rain. Not that the rain has ever stopped us, has it?" He winked at Joan.

"Are you thinking about that thunderstorm when we were on Brighton Pier? That was a day to remember. There was torrential rain that day, along with thunder and lightning. All the sensible people were indoors. Only the fools were out in it, including us." She smiled at Howard. "But that was a magical dance. The dark skies and pouring rain made it more bewitching. And I had Howard to keep me warm."

Again, Becky's imagination conjured up the lovely couple dancing alone at the end of a pier as lightning flashed through the skies. She felt Robin looking her way. He was smiling gently. She returned his smile, her glance lingering for a few seconds.

Joan and Howard talked some more about their pier adventures. Becky was thankful she was recording the conversation because she wasn't paying the couple much attention. It was hard to when she felt Robin looking at her now and again. It made her feel warm inside. She couldn't resist glancing at him too. He really did have the nicest eyes.

She jumped when Joan said loudly, "So, you'll do that for us, then?"

"Pardon?" Becky asked.

"You'll go down to the pier and dance with Robin there."

"Why would we do that?"

"So we can see if there's enough room for us to dance," Joan said with a big smile.

Becky frowned. "But don't you already know that? You danced there years ago."

"But it's all a blur to me now. I want to see how a young couple looks when they're dancing up there. And I...I..." She began to get flustered.

Howard came to her rescue. "We'd like to see if you've picked up the dance steps correctly."

"We can show you our dancing here," Becky said. She wasn't convinced by any of their reasons as to why she should go to the pier with Robin.

Robin stood up and said, "I'd like to have a dance on the pier. It's a lovely day for it. What do you say, Becky? Will you dance with me on the pier?"

Heat rushed through Becky, and all logic left her head. All of a sudden, she couldn't think of anything better she'd like to do. "Yes, I'd love that."

A short while later, she was in Robin's arms as they moved around the end of the pier. He'd set up a playlist on his phone, and the delightful music washed over them. They were getting curious looks from other visitors to the pier, but they ignored them. Joan and Howard still refused to go onto the pier until it was their actual anniversary, and so they watched from afar.

The outside world disappeared as Becky got lost in the magic of being in Robin's arms.

Everything was utterly perfect until Robin stopped dancing, and said, "We really have to talk."

Then he told her something which caused her to flee from the pier in horror.

Chapter 16

BECKY

ANGRY TEARS STUNG HER eyes. Becky wiped them away as she fled from the pier. She heard Robin calling her name but she ignored him.

How could he lie to her? Why didn't he tell her the truth yesterday? He was just like all the other men she'd been involved with. They all lied one way or another. He'd had plenty of opportunities to tell her why he was really here. She'd talked about the pier many times and he could have said something then. He should have mentioned something as soon as they'd first met! If he had, what would she have done? Would she have still got to know him? Would she have these feelings for him?

Becky kept running all the way home. She needed to be inside. Away from the world. She wanted to process her feelings. Alone.

As soon as she rushed into her house, she closed the door behind her and locked it. She leaned against the door and allowed her angry tears to fall.

Less than fifteen minutes ago, everything had been wonderful. She'd been dancing with Robin. It had felt so right to be in his arms. Like she belonged there. As if they'd been waiting for each other. She had lowered her defences and allowed herself to hope there could be something special between them. She had looked into his eyes as they'd danced. And the way he'd looked back at her made her feel so special.

But that magical moment had been destroyed by Robin.

She couldn't stop thinking about his words, and how casually he'd said them.

She closed her eyes as their horrible conversation came back to her.

He was going to destroy the pier. Oh, he hadn't used those words. He'd said it was a shame the pier was going to be dismantled soon. Those words had struck fear into her heart. She had immediately stopped dancing, removed herself from his arms, and asked him to explain. He had then said the pier was in need of a lot of repairs, but that work would cost too much. It would be more economical to dismantle it.

When she'd asked how he knew these things, he explained it was his job to know. He'd been doing survey work on the pier, and his findings showed how extensive the damage to the pier was. He'd started to go into detail, but Becky hadn't been able to take in his words. All she could do was stare at him in horror. She did manage to ask him why he hadn't told her this when they'd first met. His reply was that he hadn't found the right opportunity to do so.

And that's when she'd run away from him because she couldn't bear to look at him a moment longer.

She opened her eyes and dashed her tears away. She wasn't going to cry over him. He didn't deserve her tears. No man did.

She walked into her kitchen and made herself a strong cup of tea. Tea always made things seem better. Her hands shook as she filled the kettle with water. She was furious with Robin and his lies. A part of her mind tried to say that he hadn't lied as such, he'd just not told her the truth. She angrily told that part of her mind to shut up and leave her alone.

After switching the kettle on, Becky grabbed a packet of biscuits from the cupboard and tore it open. She shoved a chocolate chip cookie into her mouth and chomped on it. Whoever said you couldn't eat your feelings didn't know what they were talking about. She was already starting to feel better. A little.

Her attention went to the window. Her heart sank. The pier. The lovely pier. How could someone even think of destroying that beautiful structure? What would the town be without it? How would she be without it? It was too horrible to think about.

Becky made herself an extra-strong cup of tea and headed into the living room. She took the packet of biscuits with her. She was going to need them.

She sat on the sofa and opened her laptop. She needed a clear head to think about the pier. There was no way she was going to let it be destroyed. No way at all. She opened up a blank document on her computer and began to brainstorm.

Robin said the pier needed repairs. What were those repairs exactly? And how much would they cost? Was it something the town council could fund?

Oh! The town council. They could help. Surely. She should talk to them.

Becky paused in her typing. Roberta Wainwright was the mayor. She had talked to Robin yesterday about checking his background. And then about dealing with his invoices. What did that mean?

She didn't think her heart could sink any lower, but it did as she realised Roberta could have asked Robin to look at the pier on behalf of the council. But surely Roberta wouldn't agree to dismantling the pier? Even if the repairs cost more than the demolition costs? Roberta wouldn't agree to that, would she?

Fresh tears came to Becky's eyes. That's exactly what Roberta would do. She was frugal when it came to council funds. There was no way Roberta could justify spending a lot of money on repairing the old pier. Not when it was cheaper to take it down.

Becky cradled the cup in her hands and leaned back on the sofa. Was this really happening? Was her lovely pier going to be destroyed? Hopelessness washed through her.

Her chin trembled, but she refused to cry.

There must be something she could do.

There must be.

Chapter 17

ROBIN

ROBIN LEANED AGAINST the metal railings of the pier and stared out to sea. He couldn't get Becky's distressed face from his mind. Everything had gone from wonderful to disaster in less than fifteen minutes. He could still recall the amazing feeling of having Becky in his arms as they danced. She felt so right there, and he could have danced for the rest of the day.

But then he'd told her about the pier. And he'd told her in a really stupid way. He'd just blurted it out. In his mind, he'd planned a whole speech for her. There were going to be lots of details about the structure of the pier, its age, and how it was listing to one side. Then he was going to explain what repairs needed doing, and how much they would cost. And once she realised how much that was, his explanation of how it would be better to take the pier down would have been more easily accepted by Becky.

That had been his plan. But being the fool that he was, he'd made a mess of it. He didn't blame her for running off. He'd run after her and called out her name, but she hadn't stopped. She had sped up and didn't stop running as she got lost in the streets ahead.

She was never going to talk to him again. He didn't blame her. He'd handled the whole situation very badly. When they'd first met, he should have explained why he was there. Perhaps they could have had a civilised conversation about it, and then they could still have spent some time together.

Robin shook his head. Knowing how Becky felt about the pier, if he'd have told her about his job when they'd first met, she would have looked at him as if he were the devil. They wouldn't have spent time together. They wouldn't have danced together. He wouldn't have all these feelings for her.

He looked down at the railings. Bits of paint were flaking off. He picked at a loose bit. The pier was over a hundred years old. It was a miracle it had survived this long. He'd looked into the council records and discovered that very little maintenance work had been carried out on it over the years. The railings had been painted a few times, and some of the wooden boards had been replaced. But no one had given the structure a thorough examination to see what was going on. Until Roberta had hired him. Now that he had his reports, his findings couldn't be ignored.

He was only doing his job. It wasn't his fault this ancient pier was falling to pieces! He hadn't personally gone underwater and caused the legs of the structure to wear out.

Those thoughts didn't make his heart feel any better. He'd upset Becky, and nothing else mattered.

There was nothing he could do about that. Not yet. Perhaps he could try to explain himself to her later. If she would listen to him, that is.

He took one last look at the sea before turning his back on it.

His report was ready to send to Roberta Wainwright. He already knew what her decision was because she'd made that clear when she'd hired him last month. She said if the repairs were too much, she had no qualms about taking the pier down. She had added that sentimental people in the town might object, but they'd have to deal with it.

Robin's jaw set in a determined line as he came to a decision. He would send the report to Roberta and then he'd leave town. He would totally ignore his feelings for Becky. In time, he'd forget about her. He could do that.

With firm resolve in his heart, he walked along the pier and towards the promenade at the end.

Becky was waiting for him.

Chapter 18

BECKY

ROBIN SMILED AT HER and said, "Hi."

She tried to harden her heart against him. He could stop right now with his 'Hi' and his twinkling eyes. "Hello," she said as firmly as she could.

He moved closer to her and held his hands out. "Becky, can we talk? I'd like to explain myself better. I didn't give you the full details earlier."

Keeping her tone cool, she said, "I do want the full details. I want to know what repairs are needed, and how much they will cost."

"Okay." He gave her a wary look. "Why do you need those details?"

She lifted her chin. "Because I'm going to save this pier."

"How?"

"I don't know yet, but I'll do it." She looked away from his concerned face. "I'll find a way. Somehow. I won't let you destroy the pier."

"Becky, it's not me who's going to destroy the pier. It's not actually going to be destroyed, it's going to be dismantled."

Becky looked back at him. "Using a different word doesn't make it any better!"

He ran a hand over the back of his neck. "I know it doesn't. We might be able to recycle some parts of it."

"Recycle?" Becky's voice rose. "Recycle? What do you mean by that?"

Robin rubbed his neck some more as if trying to soothe himself. "Erm. Some of the wooden planks can be used on other piers which need small repairs. And not all of the metal railings have been corroded. They could be used for ornamental purposes. Perhaps in someone's garden. There's a market for that sort of thing."

Becky blanched. "You're going to rip my lovely pier apart and then cast its remains recklessly around the country!"

Robin gulped. "Well, yes. That's what we've done with other piers."

Becky was almost shouting now. "You've destroyed other piers? You've broken other hearts? You've devastated other towns? What kind of a pier-wrecking monster are you? Is this your life's mission? Does it make you happy? Do you have a chart somewhere with pictures of all the piers you've killed? Do you? Do you?"

Passers-by were stopping to stare at Becky, but she didn't care. She couldn't believe she had feelings for this heartless man. Fury was coursing through her. Look at him, standing there with his brown floppy hair.

"Becky, please. Stop shouting. Let me explain."

A horrific thought crashed into her mind. "Did you get to know me just so you could have more information about the pier? Were you sussing me out to see how I'd feel about your plans before you told anyone else? Was I a guinea pig for the rest of the town? Is that why you wanted to spend so much time with me?"

"No. No! I...I..." He was a loss for words.

And quite rightly too, Becky surmised. She had discovered his ulterior motive. She'd taken off his handsome mask and seen the pier-wrecking monster underneath.

He was saying something, but Becky refused to listen to his lies and excuses. She held her hand up to stop his words. "I would like a full copy of your report about the pier. ASAP. That means as soon as possible."

"I know what it means," he mumbled.

"Can you email me the report today?" Without waiting for his answer, she shoved her business card at him. "Here's my work email. I expect the report without delay. Can you do that? Or have you got some other piers you need to tear down?"

A cold look came into his eyes which startled Becky. "You can have my report within the hour. I'm telling you now that the pier can't be saved."

"It can." Becky blinked quickly as her eyes smarted with the threat of tears. She so did not want to cry in front of Robin. "The pier can be saved."

Keeping her head high, she walked away from him.

Despite her bravado, there was an awful feeling in her heart that the pier was beyond saving.

Chapter 19

ROBIN

HE WATCHED BECKY WALK away.

So, that's how it was going to be.

She wasn't prepared to listen to a word he said.

She'd made her mind up about him and was ready to think the worst.

She wasn't the woman he thought she was.

Well, that was okay.

It was fine.

He could live with that.

It didn't matter to him.

Not one little bit.

He looked at the business card. His report was none of her business. He was only going to send it to her because it would be publically available as soon as he sent it to Roberta. The mayor had insisted on it, and said she would put the report on the council website so the whole town could look at it. She didn't want to keep any secrets from them.

Robin quickly sent the report to the mayor. Then he sent one to Becky with the message section remaining empty.

He put his phone away. That was it, then. He'd done his job. And now he could leave this town behind.

And he could leave Becky behind too.

She didn't mean anything to him.

She didn't mean anything at all.

With those lies laying heavily in his heart, Robin walked away from the old pier.

Chapter 20

BECKY

"HOW MUCH?" BECKY EXCLAIMED to herself as she read Robin's report. "That can't be right. There must be a mistake." She read the report again hoping she'd mistaken some of the numbers.

She hadn't.

Wow.

That was a lot of money.

She put the report on the sofa. After she'd spoken to Robin earlier, she had headed in the direction of her office intending to work there for the rest of the day, but had then changed her mind. Her foolish tears kept threatening to appear, and she didn't want to fall to pieces in front of the lovely people she worked with. And one of the advantages of being a reporter meant she was able to work from home whenever she needed to.

Working alone at home didn't stop her from talking to herself, though. "He must have got his figures wrong. He must have."

She went online and checked the prices of treated wooden planks. Robin had put the precise measurements in his report, so that helped her to find the costs.

She let out a low whistle. That was a lot. Okay. So maybe that part of his report was accurate. But what about replacing the metal railings?

There was no way they could cost that much. They weren't coated in gold. She made some more online investigations.

Her eyes widened. Blimey. Who knew they could cost so much?

Becky didn't bother double-checking the rest of the work which would be needed. There was no point. She could now see Robin's report was a fair estimate of the repair work.

She picked the report up and braced herself to look at the second part of it. She hadn't dared look at it yet.

Narrowing her eyes as if that would make it easier, she read the costs involved in dismantling the pier.

It was a much smaller amount compared to the repair costs, and the work would take less than a day.

Becky felt like her heart was breaking. How could this be happening? It was like being in the middle of a nightmare, and one she couldn't wake up from.

She took a few minutes to wallow in self-pity, then she gave herself a firm talking to.

"Okay, so now we know the worst. That's good. We know what we're dealing with. Let's think about what we can do. Obviously, we want to repair the pier. And that takes money. So, we need to raise the money. That's all. Simple."

Keeping her spirits as high as she possibly could, Becky searched how to raise money. Oh, that was good. Lots of suggestions came up. Becky scrolled through them.

Garage sales. Good idea but she didn't have a garage.

A bake sale. She pulled a face. She was a terrible baker.

Car wash. Okay, that was something she could do.

Boat wash. Ah, that would be possible. There were a lot of boats around the bay.

A sponsored walk. She'd have to walk hundreds of miles to make a decent amount, but it could be done.

Sports events. That could take too much organising.

Cleaning services. Cleaning services? How was she to raise a huge amount of money doing that?

Online raffles. She glanced around her living room. Did she have anything worth raffling?

Her hopeful spirit deflated by the second.

Perhaps a dilapidated pier had somewhere in the world had been saved by someone plucky. Yes, that could have happened. People loved piers, and they would do anything to save them. There could be a convenient report online showing how funds had been raised.

With a smile on her face, Becky confidentially searched for towns who had saved the life of their beloved piers.

Within seconds, her smile vanished.

There were no heart-warming tales of towns which had come to the last-minute rescue of their piers. Not one single story.

But she found some horrific footage of a pier being dismantled at a nearby seaside town. When she saw the video come up on the search page, she didn't want to click on the play button, but she just couldn't help herself. In dramatic black and white footage, and with sad music playing, the video showed the pier being taken apart bit by bit until only a ghostly carcass was left to rot in the sea. It reminded Becky of a particular horror film she'd seen where a pack of vultures had attacked a— She shook her head, unable to let the memory play out.

Is that what Robin intended to do to her pier? Leave some of it behind to mock her?

A stubborn bubble of hope surfaced in her.

The residents of this town wouldn't stand by and let this awful thing happen. She knew them so well, and she was certain they would do everything they could to help.

Of course they would!

Once they knew about the pier's plight, some clever resident would come up with an amazing money-making idea which would more than cover the cost of repairs.

Yes, that could happen. Becky nodded to herself with conviction as if that would make it come true.

She stood up with renewed determination. She had a plan. But how could she let everyone know what was happening to the pier?

An online article? Maybe, but that would take too long because she always had to get her reports approved by her editor. And sometimes Gary took forever to do that. She could go around the town and talk to people. But that would take too long as well.

How could she get everyone together all at once?

A town meeting! Of course.

She would call a town meeting. Any resident was able to do that. Becky realised Roberta would probably object to plans to save the pier rather than demolish it, but wasn't that only if council money was used? If Becky came up with another way to raise the funds, then Roberta couldn't object. Could she?

Becky had to try.

She left her house and headed in the direction of the town hall. As she turned a corner, she came across Howard and Joan.

Joan's face was full of consternation. "Becky, love, what's happened between you and Robin? You were having such a lovely dance earlier and then you went running off. Did you have an argument?"

"We had a disagreement," Becky said, not wanting to get into the full details at the moment.

Joan put her hand on Becky's arm. "I'm sure it's nothing that can't be sorted out. You two are meant to be together. I just know you are. Can't you sort things out? Why don't you go and talk to him at the hotel?"

"I'm not going to talk to him," Becky said firmly. "Our disagreement concerns him wanting to tear our lovely pier to pieces. I've nothing to say to him." She gently pulled her arm free and began to walk away.

Joan called after her, "Talk to him!"

"No," Becky looked over her shoulder as she strode away. "I never want to see him again! I wish I'd never met Robin Hartman! I hate him!"

She turned her head back and walked straight into Robin.

Chapter 21

ROBIN

ROBIN'S ARMS INSTINCTIVELY wrapped around Becky, and for a split-second, he felt an immense sense of happiness.

But it didn't last long because Becky yelled, "Get off me!" She moved out of his arms and glowered at him. "Are you following me?"

"No. How could I be following you when it was you who walked into me?"

"I did not!"

"Yes, you did. You came storming around that corner and bashed into me. Ask Joan and Howard. They saw everything." Robin pointed to the couple. Joan and Howard immediately turned around and rushed away. "Thanks for your support!" Robin shouted after them.

When he looked back at Becky, he was surprised to see a pink tint in her cheeks. She muttered, "I didn't mean it."

"Mean what?"

"Mean what I just said." Her cheeks reddened some more. "Before I bumped into you."

The corner of Robin's mouth twitched. "So, you admit you bumped into me?"

"That's not important right now. Did you hear what I was saying before that?" She focused her attention on his left shoulder.

"That you wished you'd never met me. And that you hate me? Yes, I did hear those words."

"I didn't mean them." She was still talking to his shoulder. "I was angry with you. I still am."

"I know. I don't blame you. I'd be angry at me too. In fact, I'm furious with myself about how I've treated you." Using one hand, he swiftly typed something on his phone. "Furious. Enraged. Incensed. Outraged. I'm in a frenzy with myself. I'm incandescent with rage."

Becky looked up from his shoulder. "Hey! What are you doing?" He held his phone up so she could see the screen. "Are you looking at a thesaurus?"

"I am. I wanted to convey how angry I am with myself. Hang on, there are a few more words I could use."

Becky smiled at him, and just as suddenly, her smile fled as if realising it had no place on her face at the present moment. "You fool."

"I am. An idiot. A nincompoop. A ninny. Numpty. A pudding-head. Oh, I've not heard that expression before."

Becky started laughing. "Put the thesaurus away. I'm trying to apologise for saying those mean things."

Robin frowned. "Why are you apologising?"

She let out a sigh. "It's suddenly occurred to me that none of this is your fault. You're only doing your job. I'm assuming Roberta hired you to look at the pier."

"She did. She was worried about how much it was leaning to one side. She had concerns over health and safety issues."

Becky nodded. "I can understand that. Roberta only wants what's best for the town."

"She does. But that doesn't stop me from feeling bad about how I treated you. I know how much the pier means to you. I should have chosen my earlier words more carefully."

Becky gave him a sad smile. "You could have written the words on an enormous chocolate cake and have it delivered by sparkling fairies on the back of flying unicorns, and it wouldn't have made the information any easier to accept."

Robin couldn't help himself from moving a little closer to her. "I'm right out of sparkling fairies. And my flying unicorns are busy delivering messages to the choir of singing dragons in the mountains."

Becky burst into laughter. "Oh! You!" Her laughter subsided as she gazed into his eyes.

Robin's treacherous heart began to thud in his chest. He moved closer still until he became aware of her rose-scented perfume. "Becky?"

"Yes?"

His attention went to her lips. "I wish none of this had happened. I don't mean the meeting you part. I'm glad I met you."

"I'm glad I met you, too."

Time stood still as they looked at each other. Robin was certain he'd forgotten how to breathe.

"Robin?"

"Yes?"

"Is there anything we can do to save the pier? Do you know of any cases where a pier has been saved?"

As he looked into her beautiful eyes, he wished more than anything he could offer her a solution. "No. I'm sorry. Nothing can be done to save it."

She lowered her eyes and took a step back. "I just can't accept that. I have to do something. I have to try to save it."

"There's no point. Don't waste your time. The pier's not worth it." As soon as he'd said the words, he regretted it.

Resignation settled on Becky's face. "I have to try. Sorry for bothering you. Goodbye."

Chapter 22

BECKY

WITH A DESPONDENT HEART, Becky walked towards the town hall. When she'd asked Robin if there was anything they could do to save the pier, she'd been hoping he would come up with a marvellous plan which would immediately solve their problem. Then she would have flung herself into his arms and thanked him. Maybe she would have even kissed him.

But he hadn't come up with a plan. Not only that, he'd told her not to waste her time trying to save the pier. He had no sympathy for her. He didn't understand her at all. And she'd foolishly believed there had been a connection between them. She was so sick and tired of her heart betraying her when it came to love. She was going to stop listening to it and pay attention to her head instead.

Her head was telling her to go down every avenue possible to save her beloved pier. And the first avenue would start with the mayor of this town.

A short while later, Becky entered the town hall. She knew where Roberta Wainwright's office was because she'd been there a few times. Roberta claimed she operated under an 'open door' policy, but that wasn't the case today. Her door was closed which either meant she had a resident inside with her, or she'd left the building. Not feeling the slightest bit embarrassed, Becky put her ear against the wooden door and listened for any talking. She didn't hear any conversations, but she did hear Roberta laughing. It was such an unfamiliar sound that Becky thought she'd misheard it. But no, there it was again.

Becky knocked loudly on the door. Roberta called out for her to enter. When Becky did, she was astonished to see Roberta laughing at something on the computer screen in front of her.

Roberta cast a glance at Becky before pointing to the screen and saying, "Look at these dogs! They're trying to get impossibly long sticks through a door! They're hilarious. They keep trying even when it doesn't work. Come over here and have a look."

Becky couldn't have been more surprised if Roberta had started juggling swords. She had never seen this side of the mayor before. She moved over to Roberta's side and watched the video of a determined Labrador as he attempted a seemingly impossible feat.

Roberta wagged her finger at the dog. "Turn it around! It'll fit through that way."

Almost as if he'd heard her words, the dog repositioned himself until he could fit through the door with his stick still held tightly in his mouth. As soon as he'd got through, the dog dropped the stick and wagged his tail enthusiastically.

Roberta burst into applause. "Bravo little fella! Bravo." She clicked on the keyboard. "Watch this one, Becky. It's a similar stick situation but the dog gets help this time."

Becky was intrigued and looked closer at the screen. The dog was struggling to get through an open gate in a garden. Another dog came along and grabbed the other end of the stick in his mouth. Together, the dogs successfully lifted the stick up and over the gate.

"Teamwork," Roberta announced. "Things get done more quickly when you work as a team. Fun time over." She turned away from the computer. "What can I help you with? Take a seat."

Becky sat opposite the mayor who didn't seem so intimidating anymore. "It's the pier."

"The pier?"

"Yes. I know about it."

"Know about it?"

"Yes. I've read Robin's report."

"Robin's report?"

Becky frowned. "Are you going to repeat everything I say?" She immediately regretted her harsh words. "Sorry. I know about the pier, and the plans to destroy it."

A stern look came over Roberta's face. It was a look Becky was more familiar with. "Destroy is a harsh word. I prefer dismantling. How do you know about it? I haven't made it public yet."

Despite his insensitive words about her wasting time trying to save the pier, Becky didn't want to get Robin into trouble with the mayor. "That doesn't matter. We can't lose the pier. It means too much to the town."

"Health and safety mean much more."

"But the pier is safe. I've been on it today. And so have other people."

Roberta looked at the clock on the wall. "It's going to be cordoned off soon. I can't have anyone else going on it."

"Why? It's not falling down. Is it?"

"No, it's not that. People need to get used to not going on it. The sooner, the better. And the dismantling process will begin soon, so we might as well get the wheels in motion by cordoning it off today."

Fear gripped Becky. "No! You can't cordon it off! People should be allowed to go on it."

Roberta shrugged. "As I said, they'll have to get used to not going on it. I don't know why you're so upset. It's just a load of wooden planks and metal railings."

Becky stood up. "It isn't! It's much more than that. It's an important part of this town!" She wanted to say a lot more, but the lump in her throat stopped her.

A hint of steel came into Roberta's eyes. "I'd appreciate it if you'd lower your voice. You've read the report. You know how much repair work is needed. The council doesn't have that sort of money. Dismantling the pier is the only option."

"But what about the shopkeepers on the pier? And the people who run the amusements? And the gift shops? What's going to happen to them?"

"I'll find alternative arrangements for them. They won't lose their livelihoods." Her look softened. "Becky, you must know that dismantling is the sensible option. In fact, it's the only option."

"No. It isn't. The pier can be repaired. It can be saved." Becky's chin lifted in defiance.

"Who's going to save it?"

"Me."

"How?"

Becky's chin lowered slightly. "I don't know yet. I want to hold a town meeting."

"Why? What good will that do?"

"I don't know." Becky pointed at the mayor's computer. "A team of people might be able to think of something. You said that things get done quicker when you work as a team."

Roberta gave Becky a long look. "Okay. You can have your town meeting. I'll get the ball rolling on that. But the meeting will have to be today. Preferably this afternoon."

"Why so soon?"

Roberta paused a moment before saying, "The pier is going to be dismantled in two days."

Chapter 23

ROBIN

ROBIN SILENTLY BERATED himself as he drove back to the hotel. Why had he said those harsh words to Becky about wasting her time? He replayed the conversation yet again in his mind. He wished so much that he could have come up with a brilliant plan. One that would save the pier. Then Becky might have thrown her arms around him. They might have even kissed. He could have been her knight in shining armour. Or rather, her hero in jeans and a shirt.

But no, he'd been an insensitive idiot instead. His words had caused her such pain that it made his heart ache. He never wanted to cause her such hurt again. The only way he could do that was by not seeing her. Ever. That would cause him pain, but he'd rather be the one who was hurting rather than her.

He parked in the hotel's car park, picked up his briefcase, and left the car. His feet felt like they were made of lead as he dragged himself towards the entrance. Even though his hotel room was booked for another week, he was going to pack his suitcases and leave today. He'd delivered his report to Roberta Wainwright. There was nothing left for him to do. And he wanted to be away from Becky before his careless thoughts and actions hurt her further.

Joan and Howard were coming out of the hotel. Their faces lit up in greeting when they saw him. Robin sighed quietly. The last thing he needed was to see a loved-up couple. Joan had that look on her face which meant she wanted to stop and have a chat. He wasn't in the mood for chatting to anyone. Perhaps he should pretend to be in a hurry.

"Robin! Hello!" Joan cried out as he came closer.

He put his head down. "Hello. I can't stop. Got things to do."

Joan was having none of it. She swiftly grabbed his elbow, causing him to slow down. "We need to talk about Becky."

The mention of Becky's name made Robin come to a standstill. "Becky? What about her? Has something happened to her? Where is she?"

"Calm down. Nothing's happened to her," Joan said. "She's mad at you over the whole pier business, but it won't last."

"It will. She's never going to speak to me again."

"She will. You'll see." She shared a soft look with Howard. "People have arguments, but they make up. You need to talk to each other. Clear up any misunderstandings."

"We haven't misunderstood each other. I kept something important from her. Now, she knows the truth. We can't talk to each other because every time she looks at me, she'll think about that pier she loves so much. I can't bear to see the hurt in her eyes. We're better off apart. If you'll excuse me, I've got work to do." He took a step forward.

"But Robin," Joan began, "you and Becky have to talk. You're meant to be together. I just know you are. I've seen how you look at each other. It's destiny."

Robin shook his head. "You're wrong. So very wrong."

"Now look here, lad," Howard thundered making Robin jump. "If my wife thinks you and that lovely lass are meant to be together, then you are! She's never been wrong about these things. Never."

"She could be this time," Robin argued.

Howard's tone softened. "She isn't. And if you search your heart, you'll know that. You've fallen in love with Becky. Admit it."

Robin shrugged helplessly. "So what if I have? I'll get over it."

Howard shook his head sadly. "Love isn't like the flu. You can't get over it. I tried it with my Joan, but it didn't work. I fell madly and deeply in love with her from the moment I saw her. I tried to ignore my feelings, but I just couldn't. I'm still deeply in love with her. She means the world to me."

Robin heaved a big sigh which felt like it came all the way from his feet. "Okay, I do love Becky. I admit it. But what can I do? Nothing, that's what. She's better off without me. She'll never forgive me for what I've done. And I don't blame her."

"You're not giving her any credit, lad. She knows none of this is your fault. Joan's right about you two needing to talk. Talk and sort things out."

"She won't want to talk to me."

Howard smiled. "But she'll want to talk to me and Joan. Leave everything to me. I have a plan."

Chapter 24

BECKY

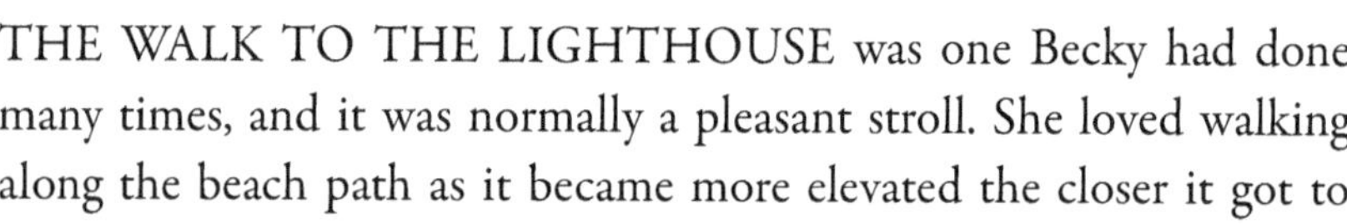

THE WALK TO THE LIGHTHOUSE was one Becky had done many times, and it was normally a pleasant stroll. She loved walking along the beach path as it became more elevated the closer it got to the lighthouse. The spectacular view of the bay revealed itself with each step taken.

But she was not enjoying the walk today. She knew from the tone of Joan's voice when she'd phoned her thirty minutes ago that something was going on. Joan had made some excuse about needing to meet Becky at the lighthouse. She'd explained there was something important which Becky needed to hear which concerned Joan and Howard's past. As much as she wanted to write the couple's story, all of Becky's thoughts were focused on the pier, and how it was going to be torn down in two days.

Two days. Oh. Becky's steps slowed. That was Joan and Howard's anniversary. They were planning to dance on the pier with all their friends and family watching. But the pier was going to be closed. Joan and Howard probably didn't know that yet. Becky didn't want to be the one to tell them. But they had to know. They would have to make alternative arrangements. Or cancel everything.

That was so sad. Becky cast a backward look at the bay. She could see the pier in all its glory. What was the view going to be like without it? Tears came to her eyes. The tears weren't for her this time. They were for Joan and Howard. She wanted them to have the celebration they deserved. She might not be able to save the pier, but could she make sure Joan and Howard still got to dance on it before it was destroyed? Surely Roberta would allow that?

She carried on walking and had an imaginary conversation with Roberta in which she convinced the major to allow the anniversary celebrations to go ahead. Becky was so lost in her thoughts that she didn't notice someone was walking behind her. She only became aware when she saw his shadow merging with hers. The familiar scent of his aftershave came to her.

"Hello," she said to Robin as he joined her. She gave him the briefest of smiles.

"Hi." His reply was guarded.

They walked on in silence for a while, their steps in sync with each other.

The silence was heavy between them.

Becky couldn't bear it another moment. "Where are you going?"

"To the lighthouse," he replied. "Where are you going?"

"The lighthouse." Becky stopped walking. Robin did too. "Why are you going there?"

"Because Howard and Joan asked me to. Why are you going?"

"The same reason as you. Joan said she wanted to tell me more of their story. Why do they want you there?" Her eyes widened. "Oh! That sounded awful. I didn't mean it that way."

Robin smiled warmly making him look far too handsome. Butterflies fluttered in her stomach. She mentally told them to behave. Robin said, "The same reason as you. I would like to know what their full story is too. We keep getting snippets, but not the full thing. It must be annoying for you because you can't write your article yet. And frustrating."

She was touched by his concern. "I've dealt with worse." They started walking again. "I had an elderly woman contact me once. She wanted to come clean about some crimes she'd committed in her youth. She'd got away with them, but guilt had caught up with her in her later years. She wanted to make a public confession via the newspaper."

"What were her crimes?"

"Well, that's the thing. I never found out. When I first visited her, she had three notebooks in front of her. I assumed they were full of the crimes she'd committed."

"Three notebooks?"

Becky laughed. "Yes. That was a worry. When I saw them, I thought I was dealing with a master criminal. She insisted on making me a cup of tea before I interviewed her. She took the notebooks into the kitchen with her. A minute later, I heard the back door opening." Becky shook her head at the memory. "She did a runner. And took her books with her."

"No! She didn't!" Robin started to laugh.

"She certainly did. I waited for about thirty minutes. I phoned her, but she'd left her mobile in the living room. I asked her neighbours where she was. They said she often took off at a moment's notice and could be gone for weeks."

"What did you do?"

"I left. But then she phoned me a few days later. She apologised and said she'd had cold feet about confessing. She said after some careful thought, she was ready to talk to me. So, off I went again." Becky smiled at Robin. "Guess what happened?"

"She ran off again?"

Becky nodded. "She did. This happened three more times before I said no to any further home visits. And I said if she wanted to talk to me, she would have to come to the newspaper office. I see her sometimes hanging around outside the office. She looks like she's about to come in, but then she rushes off like a startled deer."

Robin shook his head as he laughed some more. "Do you think you'll ever get her story?"

Becky shrugged. "Who knows? We've got a bet on her in the office. Someone suggested contacting the police about her supposed crimes so that they could talk to her. I'm not going to be the one who phones the police. She could be making it all up as far as I know."

As they carried on walking, Robin asked her about the strangest stories she'd ever covered. Becky had plenty of those to tell him and proceeded to regale him with the more obscure articles she'd written.

Robin was a good listener. He was good company, too. Becky was in a much better mood by the time they reached the lighthouse.

Howard and Joan were sitting on a bench holding hands. They smiled over at Robin and Becky as they approached.

"Hello!" Joan called out. "Isn't it a lovely day? Look at this amazing view. Doesn't the air feel fresher up here? Sit yourselves down on that bench."

Becky sat at one side of the bench, and Robin sat at the other.

Joan glanced at the space between Becky and Robin but she didn't say anything. She shared a look with Howard. He nodded.

Joan looked out to sea one more time before turning to Becky and saying, "It's time you knew the truth about Howard and me."

Chapter 25

HOWARD AND JOAN

JOAN SAID, "AS YOU know, I grew up in Holly Blue Bay. I love this town and thought I'd never leave it."

Becky smiled at that.

Joan continued, "I was working at the Holly Blue Hotel when I met Howard. I think I told you before that I was twenty-four. I worked with a great group of people. We had lots of nights out including those dances at the church hall. I was single, and happy to be so. But then I met this fella, and my life changed." She smiled up at Howard. "For the better. I was so happy. After meeting at the church hall, Howard and I went on dates, and I felt like we were going to be together for the rest of our lives."

"But something happened, something terrible," Howard said. "Shall I tell them, my love?"

Joan nodded. "You know I don't like talking about it."

He gave her a quick kiss on the cheek. "I know you don't. I'll keep it brief. Becky, I came to Holly Blue Bay for work reasons. I'm retired now, but I used to be an engineer, just like you, Robin. I came to the town to look at some of the older buildings. Some of them needed a lot of attention. Anyway, back to me and Joan. She loved going on that pier, but I couldn't see the attraction in it. There were plenty of kiosks on it but most of them were empty. The pier felt like a dismal, unloved place to me. And I foolishly said that to Joan. Even worse, I said the pier looked dilapidated and it should be taken down. I called it an eyesore."

Joan said, "I nearly exploded with rage. I couldn't believe he was saying such awful things about my lovely pier. They must have heard me shouting at the other end of town. Here was this man I loved, but he was saying such awful things about the pier. I didn't understand how he could, not when he knew how much it meant to me. I thought he didn't know me at all, and he certainly didn't love me. How could he if he didn't understand me?"

Becky and Robin shared a brief look before staring intently out to sea.

"She wouldn't stop shouting," Howard said. "I tried to defend myself, but it was no good. She called me all sorts of names before storming off."

"I was determined to prove him wrong. I was going to show him how amazing the pier was." She sighed. "He was right about the empty kiosks. They were dilapidated, and businesses didn't want to set up there. I was so furious with Howard that I made it my mission to change things around."

"She was like a human tornado," Howard said. "I watched her from afar as she rallied the people of the town to do something about the pier. And they couldn't refuse her! I kept trying to apologise to her for my thoughtless remarks, but she refused to listen to me. I sent her flowers, chocolates, books, everything I could think of to apologise. But all my gifts came back to me."

"I just couldn't see sense at the time," Joan admitted. "I knew I was being pig-headed, and I knew I loved Howard, but my stubbornness wouldn't let me admit it. Poor Howard. Every time we bumped into each other, he was all smiles but I wasn't. I hate to think about that time now. I hated being apart from him."

"How long were you apart?" Becky asked.

"Too long," Howard said. "It was three excruciating months. I kept making up excuses as to why I should stay in the town. I did a lot of work on buildings which didn't even need repairs. I couldn't leave Joan. She was the love of my life, and no matter how long it took, I was going to win her back."

Joan gazed at her husband. "Tell them what you did, you big softie."

"I repaired the dilapidated kiosks. I replaced the rotten wood and fixed leaking roofs."

"He did it at night-time after he'd finished his work for the day," Joan pointed out. "And he did it free of charge. I caught him one night halfway down the pier. He was doing something to one of the kiosks. I thought he was destroying them! I marched down there and started yelling at him. He waited until I'd run out of steam and then he told me calmly what he was doing. I felt such a fool."

"A beautiful fool," Howard said with his voice full of love. "Once all the kiosks were fixed, I talked to some of the businesses around town to see if they'd be interested in moving to the pier."

Joan said, "You're not giving them the full story. You pestered them until they said yes. That's what they told me afterwards."

"I had to. I had to get them on the pier. I knew how happy that would make you. I would have done anything to make you happy." A twinkle came into his eyes. "And it worked, didn't it? When you saw the pier after it had been fixed, your face lit up. Your beauty mesmerised me. I knew I wanted to marry you."

Joan leaned her head against his shoulder. "And what a proposal it was. The music. The dancing. What a magical night it was. I can't wait to do it again."

"Me too." Howard put his arm around his wife's shoulder and pulled her closer.

Becky abruptly stood up. "I've got something to do. Something very important. Goodbye!" She raced off along the path before anyone could say another word.

Howard noticed Robin's despondent expression. "Robin, go after her. Talk to her."

"And say what?"

"Anything! Don't let her get away, lad. Go after her. Don't let this pier business get in the way of your love. It nearly did with me and my Joan."

Robin broke into a smile. "I will go after her." His phone beeped. He looked at it. His smile died. "Oh no."

"What's wrong?" Joan asked.

"It's a message from Roberta. Becky's holding a town meeting in two hours to stop the pier being dismantled. Roberta wants me to be there to show my report to everyone. She wants me to argue against Becky."

Chapter 26

BECKY

BECKY'S MOUTH FELT dry as she stood in front of a packed room at the town hall. She hadn't been expecting this many people to turn up. Roberta had sent out messages via social media about an urgent town meeting. Her messages hadn't said what the meeting was about, so Becky assumed a lot of people had turned up out of curiosity. She hoped they wouldn't be too disappointed when she started talking about the pier.

After hearing Howard and Joan's story at the lighthouse, Becky had been filled with determination to make their anniversary happen. She had immediately rushed to the town hall to speak to Roberta, but the mayor had been out on a council matter. A few minutes after hearing that news, Becky got a text message from Roberta to let her know the meeting Becky had requested was going to happen in less than two hours. It hadn't left Becky much time to prepare, but she already knew what she was going to say. She had to persuade the residents of Holly Blue Bay the pier was worth saving. And the best way to tug on their heartstrings was to tell them stories about the pier.

And here she was, with a folder full of stories, standing in front of the expectant audience.

Roberta was at Becky's side. She was telling the town's people the meeting had been called by Becky, and that it involved the pier. A surprising amount of groans came from the audience which didn't do anything for Becky's spirits. Even worse, about a dozen people stood up and left the room.

Becky noticed Robin coming into the room and taking a seat at the back. What was he doing here?

"So," Roberta announced, "it's over to you, Becky." Roberta walked away and took a seat in the front row.

The silence was deafening. All eyes were trained on her. Becky's heart sped up and her hands felt clammy. She'd never had a panic attack before and didn't know what the symptoms were. She hoped she wasn't having one now. Her throat was ridiculously dry. She took a sip of water, glancing at the rear exit doors as she did so.

Robin was looking at her with a kind smile. He gave her a double thumbs-up sign which made her smile back at him.

Becky faced the audience with as much confidence as she could muster. "Good afternoon everyone. Thank you for coming here. I appreciate it. I don't know if you're aware, but our beautiful pier is in danger. There are plans to destroy it."

"Dismantle it," Roberta called out. "We're going to dismantle it. Carry on, Becky."

Becky carried on, "I'm not going to tell you how much I love the pier, which is a lot by the way. I'm going to tell you about stories concerning other people, and how much the pier meant to them." She held her folder up. "I've been collecting articles from The Holly Blue Bay Gazette for years. I've found some older ones too. These relate to the pier. If it's okay, I'd like to read them out."

There was a murmur amongst the audience as if they were discussing it. Three more people left the room.

From the back, Robin shouted, "I'd love to hear them!"

Becky could have kissed him.

She began, "This one is from a resident called Mary Brown. She married her sweetheart, John just before the start of the first world war.

She stood at the end of the pier and watched as he sailed away. He promised to return to her and their unborn child as soon as he could. Every evening, Mary waited on the end of the pier hoping to see John returning. No matter the weather, she would stand there gazing out to sea. The only time she missed a day was when she gave birth to her daughter." Becky paused for a moment to gather herself together for the rest of the story. Some people in the audience leaned forward in their seats. "Four years passed, and still Mary went to the end of the pier. She took her daughter with her. Together, they kept their daily vigil. And one day, John came back. The first view of his daughter was her standing at the end of the pier with her mother, both madly waving at him."

There was a collective sigh of relief.

Becky held up the faded piece from the newspaper which showed the happy family.

"My next story is about Abigail Taylor who runs the gift shop on the pier. You all know Abigail."

There were nods of agreement.

Becky said, "You know she's got those magnets behind her counter, the ones from all over the world. Do you know how she started collecting them?" She saw the shaking of heads. "In her youth, Abigail travelled the world. It was after her parents died. She just up and left the town. She was gone for five years. The newspaper wrote a story about her adventures. She's done some amazing things. Bungee jumping in New Zealand. A wildlife safari in Africa. Hot air ballooning in Turkey. White water rafting in Canada. Trekking Machu Picchu. A helicopter ride over the Grand Canyon. Swimming in the Dead Sea. Sleeping under the stars in the Sahara. And so many other things that I can only dream about."

There was a suitable number of 'oohs' and aahs' from the people in front of her. Someone said, "You wouldn't think that to look at her, would you?"

Holding up a newspaper clipping of the smiling Abigail, Becky said, "She brought back magnets from her travels, but soon, she asked other people to put their travel magnets behind the counter too. When people visit from overseas, Abigail gives them Holly Blue Bay magnets to take home. She makes the magnets herself, and she doesn't charge for them. Imagine how many of them there are around the world! I've got an enlarged picture of one of her magnets here."

Becky held up a colour photo. The pier was prominent on the magnet.

She told them about other pier-related stories, most of them happy, and a few of them heart-wrenching. More than one tear was shed throughout the audience.

Becky concluded her talk by asking, "How many of you have used the pier as a meeting point? How many of you have said, 'Meet me at the pier'? I know I have."

Just about every hand was raised, including Roberta's.

"Where would our town be without the pier? Where would we meet?" She left the question hanging in the air.

Roberta spoiled the dramatic effect by standing up and saying, "People can meet by the ice cream parlour. Everyone knows where that is. Thank you, Becky. You can sit down now."

"But, I wanted to talk about raising money to repair the pier," Becky said.

Roberta walked over to Becky. "You should have started with that. People don't have all day to listen to you." She looked towards the back of the room. "Robin, it's your turn now."

Becky's brow wrinkled as she watched Robin walk to the front of the room. What was he going to say?

Chapter 27

ROBIN

ROBIN'S STEPS WERE hesitant as he made his way to the front of the room. He gripped his briefcase tightly. He didn't want to be doing this. Not after Becky's emotional speech. He hadn't realised how important the pier was to the town. How much history it had. The passion in Becky's eyes as she spoke about it made him love her even more. He was tempted to tear his report in half and then somehow find a way to save the pier.

"Robin!" Roberta snapped. "Come along. Have you got the report with you?"

"I have." Robin sped up. Becky was looking at him with a wary expression on her face. He gave her a tight-lipped smile hoping to convey this was the last thing he wanted to do. She averted her eyes and walked away from the front of the room. She took a seat at the back.

Roberta clasped her hands together and faced the seated people. "You've heard how Becky feels about the pier. Which is all well and good. But we have to consider the facts. The pier is old. It needs a lot of work. Work that the council can't afford. Dismantling it is the only option. You might have seen Robin Hartman around the town these last few days. I hired him to undertake a detailed examination of the pier. He'll now read his report to you."

She gave Robin a firm nod before returning to her seat.

Robin's throat felt dry. He wasn't sure he'd be able to read the report. He glanced at Roberta. Her impatient look didn't help his nerves. He saw a movement at the back of the hall. It was Becky. She was giving him a double thumbs-up sign and a big smile.

His heart softened. She was so lovely.

The sight of her smiling face gave him the courage he needed. He took the report from his briefcase, cleared his throat, and proceeded to read it. He was well aware his voice was flat and emotionless. He didn't care. He was there to deliver the facts, so that's what he did.

He occasionally caught Becky's eye. She had a soft smile on her face as if she was enjoying listening to him. She was the only one who was looking at him like that. Everyone else looked like they were falling asleep.

Once he'd finished reading the report, Robin put it back in his briefcase and returned to his seat which was right next to Becky's.

"I'm sorry about that," he whispered.

She shook her head. "It's not your fault. I'm sorry I've been so mean to you."

"I deserved it."

"No," she said as she gazed into eyes, "you didn't."

Robin's throat felt dry for another reason.

Roberta's voice thundered out, "There we have it. Becky wants you to put your hands in your pockets so you can pay for the pier repairs. Robin Hartman's report shows how much money that will cost. And how much the dismantling process will cost in comparison. The decision is obvious. The pier will be taken down very soon. Some of you may have already noticed it has been cordoned off. No one is to go on the pier under any circumstances. This meeting is now over."

Robin leaned closer to Becky and said, "I don't like your mayor very much."

"Me neither. Not at the moment anyway." Becky was looking at Roberta. She stood up. "Excuse me, I have to ask her something."

She walked over to Roberta who was putting her jacket on. Robin watched Becky talk to the mayor. He couldn't hear what they were saying but it was clear from their body language that Roberta was saying a firm no to whatever Becky was asking.

After a few minutes, Becky walked swiftly away from Roberta and headed for the exit. She gave Robin a wan smile of farewell before rushing out of the door. He was dismayed to see tears in her eyes.

Anger ran through Robin. What had Roberta said to Becky to upset her so much?

There was only one way to find out.

Chapter 28

BECKY

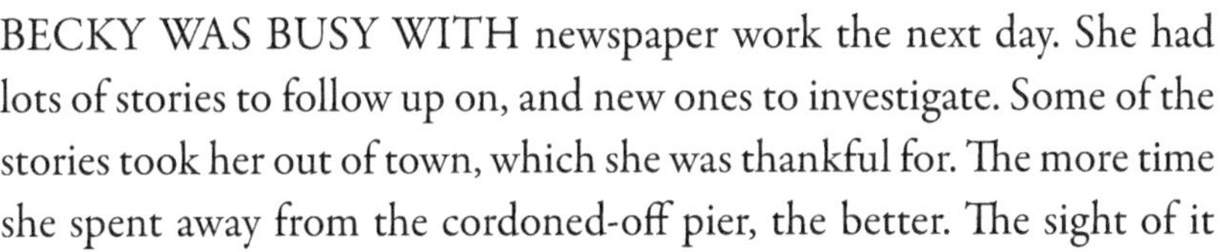

BECKY WAS BUSY WITH newspaper work the next day. She had lots of stories to follow up on, and new ones to investigate. Some of the stories took her out of town, which she was thankful for. The more time she spent away from the cordoned-off pier, the better. The sight of it made her heart feel heavy. She was tempted to leave the town for a week or more so that she wouldn't be there when the pier was destroyed.

It was early afternoon when she drove towards a farm where they'd had a bumper amount of calves born that month. She thought about her last conversation with Roberta. She had asked for the tape to be removed from the end of the pier to allow Howard and Joan to hold their anniversary celebrations. Roberta had given her an emphatic no. Becky had pleaded with her, but Roberta said she couldn't make an exception for anyone. There was a defiant look in the mayor's eyes, and Becky knew there was no point trying to argue her case.

Becky had spent the previous evening writing up Howard and Joan's story, and had wanted to end it with details of how they'd recreated their magical night on the pier. That wasn't going to happen now. She'd tried many times to phone Joan to let her know, but kept getting her answering service. She'd left a message on the service but Joan hadn't phoned her back yet. Becky had sent text messages and emails, but again, there had been nothing from Joan. Becky had phoned the hotel to see if the couple were still booked in. They were, but they were out somewhere.

Becky wondered if they knew about the pier being unavailable by now. Surely they must do. Had they made alternative arrangements? Or were they just going to head home? She felt so sorry for them. But what could she do?

She wanted to phone Robin just to hear his voice, but couldn't think of a reason to call him. She could thank him for his support last night, but was that a good enough reason?

Becky arrived at the farm and parked up. She forced personal problems out of her mind. It was time to be professional. When she'd spoken to the farmer and his wife that morning, they'd been over the moon at having so many calves born. The farmer had started to go into more detail, but Becky said she'd get the full information when she called round to see them.

The door to the farmhouse was opened the second Becky stepped out of the car. The farmer and his wife were standing there, each holding a calf in their arms. Their faces were full of such jubilation that Becky couldn't help but smile at them. This was the best part of her job. Sharing lovely stories with people. The small, everyday moments which made life so special. It was people who lived in and around the town which made Becky's days so wonderful.

Becky spent a delightful hour with the farmer and his family. She was introduced to all the calves. Each one had been named, and Becky was given the reason behind each name. She took far too many photos, but she couldn't help herself. There was so much happiness and elation on the farm. And a lot of laughter.

By the time Becky left, her spirits were as high as the blue sky above her, and thoughts of the pier were far away.

She had more delightful stories ahead of her. Becky was filled with gratitude that she got to share people's lives so intimately. She was so fortunate to have such a rewarding job.

As the day wore on, Becky found herself singing louder and louder as she drove from one home to another. It was when she finished her last visit, that she got a text from Robin.

His message was simple:

Meet me on the pier.

Chapter 29

ROBIN

ROBIN PACED BACK AND forth at the end of the pier.

Joan put her hand up to stop him. "It'll be okay," she said. "Calm down."

He stopped pacing. "I can't. I'm too nervous. Have I done the right thing? What will she say?"

"She'll be delighted."

"Will she? Or will she be annoyed? She'll think I've interfered."

"Why will she think that?" Joan asked. She beckoned Howard to come over to them.

"Because she wanted to be the one to do this." Robin glanced nervously along the pier. "I should have let her do it."

Joan gave Howard a pointed look.

Howard said, "Robin, lad, calm yourself down. What's done is done. Becky will love it. You've done this out of the kindness of your heart. She'll see that."

"Will she?" Robin pulled at the collar of his shirt. Why did it feel so tight? "Will she see that?"

"Yes, she will. Becky's got a good heart, just like my Joan." Howard pulled Joan to his side and said to her, "Have I told you today that I love you?"

"You have. Ten times or more."

"And have I told you how beautiful you are?"

Joan blushed. "You have."

Robin smiled as he looked at the loved-up couple. They'd had difficulties in the past, and they had still ended up together. Could things work out for Becky and him? He hoped so.

His phone beeped. He read Becky's reply to his earlier message. He smiled and told Howard and Joan that Becky was on her way.

He pulled at his shirt collar again. Why was it so tight?

Chapter 30

BECKY

BECKY ALMOST CRASHED her car as she drove closer to the pier. What had happened to it?

She parked in the nearby car park and got out of her car, her eyes never leaving the pier.

The tape which had cordoned it off had gone. Fairy lights had been strewn along every inch of the metal railings. Blue garlands in the shape of Holly Blue butterflies were wound around each kiosk and building. People dressed up to the nines milled around the pier as they looked at the shops and amusements.

Becky's confused thoughts couldn't make sense of any of it. What was going on? Was there a special town anniversary which she didn't know about?

She moved closer to the entrance of the pier and heard the distant strain of a familiar tune. Was it? No, it couldn't be.

Some of the people around her nodded a greeting. She knew some of them, but some were unfamiliar.

As if in a trance, Becky walked along the pier. The music got louder. It was music which she now definitely recognised.

Then she saw him.

Robin.

Like a dream, he appeared in front of her. He was wearing a black tuxedo and a white shirt. He looked impossibly handsome. His hair was smoothed back. His eyes seemed even bluer than ever as they held her gaze.

He held one hand out to her. "Becky, would you do me the honour of dancing with me?"

"What's happening?"

"I'm asking you to dance." He gave his outstretched palm a pointed look. "Don't leave me hanging."

Becky waved her hands around. "What's happened to the pier? There are people I don't know. Who are they? What's going on?"

"It's Howard and Joan's anniversary. A day early, but they're okay with that. These people are their family and friends. The deliriously happy couple are at the end of the pier in each other's arms. They are dancing. And I would like us to join them. Shall we?"

Becky put her hand in his. "I don't understand. Who did this? The decorations? The music? Who was it?"

Robin wrapped his warm fingers around her hand. "I did. Isn't it a lovely evening?"

"You did?" Becky stared at him. "How? Why? When?"

"You have a lot of questions."

"And I'd like some answers." Her tone softened. "Why did you do this, Robin?"

"Because you wanted it to happen. I spoke to Roberta last night after you'd left the hall. I convinced her to open the pier again, at least for tonight."

"You convinced her? How?"

He smiled at her. "Does it matter? Come on. I want to dance with you."

Becky wanted to dance with him too. The reporter in her had a lot more questions, but she ignored them.

Together, Becky and Robin walked along the pier until they reached the end. Howard and Joan were dancing, blissfully unaware of the world around them.

Becky gasped. "There's a band! I thought it was recorded music which was playing. Did you organise the band too?"

"I did. I know people," Robin replied with a nonchalant air. He spun her around until she was facing him. He put his other hand on her shoulder. "I hope I can remember the dance steps. I apologise now if I step on your feet."

Becky's heart was beating too fast. "The same goes for me."

Robin didn't take his eyes off her as they danced at the end of the pier. Howard and Joan noticed them after a few minutes and gave them a friendly wave which Becky and Robin were oblivious to.

They had two more dances before Becky said, "We need to talk."

"Now? What about?"

"The pier."

Robin removed his hands. "Becky, I can't tell you how sorry I am about the report, and everything else."

"I know you are. Come over here." She took his hand and walked over to the metal railings. She gazed out to sea. "This is where I was standing when I first saw your boat. I've had a good think about the pier today, and why it means so much to me. And why it means so much to everyone else too. It's not the pier. It's the events which take place on it. It's the people and the stories. The pier itself is just wood and metal. I hadn't seen it that way before. But I have now. When the pier is gone, people will still have their stories. Life will go on."

Robin said, "But you love this pier."

Becky steeled herself. She could do this. She could say this. It was the right thing to do.

She looked away from the sea and into Robin's eyes. "You mean more to me than the pier. Robin, I'm falling in love with you."

He smiled. "I'm one step ahead of you. I've already fallen in love with you."

"You have?"

"I have." He pulled her close. "I love you."

Leaning against the metal railings because her knees had suddenly gone weak, Becky's lips met Robin's.

Nearby, Joan pulled her husband's head closer and whispered in his ear, "Look at Becky and Robin. I told you I was right about them."

Howard smiled. "You're always right, my love." He looked over at the couple. "There's magic on this pier tonight. It's a shame it's going to be pulled down."

Joan said, "I wouldn't be too sure about that."

EPILOGUE

THREE MONTHS LATER

BECKY CHECKED HER WATCH as she rushed along the promenade. She was five minutes late. She frowned. She hated being late for anything. But it hadn't been her fault. The man she'd been interviewing about a story for the newspaper kept answering phone calls, which she'd thought was very rude.

"Sorry I'm late," she cried out to the man who was waiting for her.

Robin smiled. "That's okay. You're worth waiting for." He gently kissed her. "Hi."

"Hi." She smiled back at him. "How are you?"

"Same as I was yesterday. Madly in love with you."

"Oh, you!" She looked at the covered structure behind her. "Why did you want to meet me here?"

"It seemed the best place to meet."

Her nose wrinkled. "I don't like seeing the pier like this. Why is it still covered up? How long does it take to destroy it? It's been like this for months."

"Dismantle, not destroy. I told you there's been trouble with the contractors. But it's all sorted out now. The cover is coming off."

"Oh. Right. And you want me to see this?" Becky grimaced. "I know I've come to terms with it, but I don't think I'm ready to see an empty space yet. I can't imagine the pier not being here."

"You don't have to." Robin took her hand. He nodded to a man whom Becky hadn't even noticed standing just to Robin's left.

The man spoke to someone on his phone.

"What's going on?" Becky asked. "Who's that man? Who's he talking to?"

"You have too many questions. Just be patient." Robin kissed the tip of her nose.

Becky tried to be patient. She looked at the huge covering which had been in place for three months. It covered the whole of the pier right to the very end. Taking the pier down had been hard enough to deal with, but having that work delayed because of inconsiderate contractors had made it much worse.

The corner of the covering fell away. The rest of the material soon followed until it was lying in a crumpled heap.

Becky stared. Her mouth fell open. She continued to stare without blinking.

Robin gently put his index finger under her chin and closed her mouth. "Is something wrong?" he teased.

Becky pointed ahead of her. "The...the...pier...the..." Her mouth fell open again.

"Ah, yes. The pier. It's still here." Robin broke into an enormous smile. "Surprise."

"But how? When? Who? How?" She shook her head. "Robin, what's happened?"

"I raised money to repair your beloved pier. Would you like to stroll along it?"

"How did you manage to get so much money?"

Robin said, "An online campaign. I put as many pier stories as I could online, those from your newspaper clippings."

"I did wonder why you wanted those." Becky looked at the renovated pier. "You raised enough money for the pier? And without me knowing. How? I've got a Google alert for any mentions of the town."

"Ah, about that. I did sneak onto your computer and temporarily disable that alert. I hope you don't mind."

"I should, but I don't. Did people really give you money for the pier?"

"They did. Those newspaper stories affected people in a positive way. There was tremendous support for the pier. For once, stop asking questions. Come with me." He led her onto the newly replaced boards.

"It's like walking onto a brand new pier," Becky said as they strolled along. "Has this work being going on right under my nose?"

"No more questions," he reminded her. "I'm going to be the one asking questions."

Becky wondered what those questions were, but she didn't say another word as they walked side by side.

When they reached the end, Robin asked, "Where exactly were you standing when your hat blew off?"

"About here." She stood beside the freshly painted railing.

Robin moved in front of her. He got down on one knee.

"Robin, what are you—"

"No more questions. Let me ask you one. I never believed in love at first sight until the day I met you. You are the love of my life. Will you marry me?" He held a ring out. The sparkle of the diamond almost matched the twinkle in his eyes.

Becky's heart felt like it was going to melt. "Yes. Of course. Yes!"

Robin slipped the ring onto her finger. Then he picked her up and swung her around. He called out, "She said yes!"

"Who are you talking to?"

A band of musicians appeared from one of the kiosks. They began to play the song which Becky and Robin had first danced to.

"Becky, will you dance with me?"

"Always."

As the couple began to dance., a couple of Holly Blue butterflies alighted on the railings behind them. Becky and Robin were still dancing as the setting sun cast its rays across the pier in Holly Blue Bay.

A note from the author

I HOPE YOU ENJOYED this story. If you did, I'd love it if you could post a small review. Reviews really help authors to sell more books. Thank you!

This story has been checked for errors by myself and my team. If you spot anything we've missed, you can let us know by emailing us at: cathy@cathyblossom.com

WARM WISHES
Cathy Blossom

Other books by Cathy Blossom

HOLLY BLUE BAY SERIES:
    Book 1 - A Fresh Start In Holly Blue Bay
    Book 2 - Kira's Kaleidoscope
    Book 3 - A Secret Love Comes To Town
    Book 4 - Meet Me On The Pier

BILLIONAIRE ROMANCE Series:
    The Billionaire Guest - A Billionaire Clean Romance - Book 1
    The Billionaire Writer - A Billionaire Clean Romance - Book 2
    The Billionaire Movie Star - A Billionaire Clean Romance - Book 3

Meet Me On The Pier
A Holly Blue Bay Romance
(Book 4)
By
Cathy Blossom